# ≡FALL

When the bones of the Magi are stolen from their resting place in a German cathedral, the whispered words of a dying priest catapult Dane Maddock and Bones Bonebrake into the midst of a deadly race to solve a centuries-old conspiracy. Danger lurks at every turn and no one knows where the clues will lead... or what they will uncover.

From ancient cathedrals, to hidden temples, to icy mountain peaks, Maddock and Bones must outrun and outwit their enemies in the thrilling adventure- Icefall!

## PRAISE FOR DAVID WOOD
## AND THE DANE MADDOCK ADVENTURES

"Dane and Bones.... Together they're unstoppable. Rip roaring action from start to finish. Wit and humor throughout. Just one question - how soon until the next one? Because I can't wait." Graham Brown, author of Shadows of the Midnight Sun

"What an adventure! A great read that provides lots of action, and thoughtful insight as well, into strange realms that are sometimes best left unexplored." Paul Kemprecos, author of Cool Blue Tomb and the NUMA Files

"A page-turning yarn blending high action, Biblical speculation, ancient secrets, and nasty creatures. Indiana Jones better watch his back!" Jeremy Robinson, author of SecondWorld

# ICEFALL

## A DANE MADDOCK ADVENTURE

# DAVID WOOD

Icefall, A Dane Maddock Adventure
Published by Adrenaline Press
www.adrenaline.press
Adrenaline Press is an imprint of Gryphonwood Press
www.gryphonwoodpress.com
Copyright 2011, 2017 by David Wood
All rights reserved.

ISBN-10: 1-940095-62-X
ISBN-13: 978-1-940095-62-2

# BOOKS BY DAVID WOOD

*The Dane Maddock Adventures*
Dourado
Cibola
Quest
Icefall ✓
Buccaneer
Atlantis ✓
Ark
Xibalba
Solomon Key (forthcoming)

*Dane and Bones Origins*
Freedom
Hell Ship
Splashdown
Dead Ice
Liberty
Electra
Amber
Justice
Treasure of the Dead ↙

*Jade Ihara Adventures (with Sean Ellis)*
Oracle
Changeling

*Bones Bonebrake Adventures*
Primitive
The Book of Bones

*Jake Crowley Adventures (with Alan Baxter)*
Blood Codex
Anubis Key (forthcoming)

*"Then Herod called the Magi secretly and found out from them the exact time the star had appeared."*
*Matthew 2.7*

# PROLOGUE

**"They are coming** for me." Johannes had repeated the words so many times that they no longer held any meaning. It was now a mantra; sounds to ward off the shadows that lurked in the night. He no longer remembered what, exactly, he feared lurked in the darkness just beyond the edge of his vision. Bitter cold and utter exhaustion had driven that from his mind. Now, it was only the memory of fear that drove him on.

Snow crunched under his feet with each frozen footfall, a counterpoint to the steady whisper of the ice-choked Rhine. Each exhalation sent up a cloud of vapor that wreathed his face like an ethereal fog as he stumbled through the frozen night. Up ahead, a faint twinkle of lights beckoned to him. He was almost there!

Hope kindled a tiny flame somewhere deep inside him and he quickened his pace. He tightened his grip on the sack slung over his shoulder. What was inside it? He couldn't quite remember.

By the time he staggered up the cathedral steps, he scarcely had the strength to stand. He fell against the door and managed with only the greatest of efforts, to knock twice. He waited, soft flakes of snow brushing his cheeks like angel's wings. Finally, he heard a voice from inside.

"Who is there?'

"Johannes." He poured all his strength into the word, but it came out barely a murmur. The man inside must have heard him, because he continued as expected.

"And what brings you here at this hour?"

Johannes drew a shivering breath and spoke the one word that would gain him entrance.

"Dreihasenbild."

The door creaked open and he managed to take three wobbling steps inside before he fell to his knees. The cathedral was hardly warm inside, but after days trekking through the snow, it felt to Johannes like summertime. The gloved fingers of his left hand sought the clasp at the neckline of his cloak, but they were too numb to manage the task. His right hand still clutched the sack, and he would not relinquish that until he saw the priest.

"Here, brother, let us get you somewhere you can rest." Strong hands grabbed him under the arms and helped him to his feet.

"Must see the Father," he gasped. "Dreihasenbild," he added for emphasis. That should forestall any argument from the robed and hooded monk who supported his weight as he hobbled down the aisle, stopping before the altar. "Bring the Father."

"I am here." A tall man with a shaved head and amber-colored eyes seemed to materialize out of thin air. He moved to the altar and stood before Johannes. Their eyes locked, and the father's brow crinkled slightly, as if he waited for Johannes to answer a question yet unasked. "I am pleased to see you have returned safely."

Johannes found himself unable to meet the priest's gaze. His eyes drifted to the golden casket behind the altar. As his eyes locked on its shining surface, memories came flooding back. His knees gave way and he slumped to the floor.

"Johannes!" The priest dropped to one knee in front of him and clasped his shoulders. "Forgive me. I was so pleased to see you alive that I did not consider the condition you are in." He glanced up at the monk who had opened the door for Johannes. "Fetch a blanket, food, and a cup of hot water for our brother."

The monk hurried away. When the sound of his footsteps faded into silence, the priest's demeanor changed. His expression grew grave and his stare hard.

"Did you find it?" There was no need to say what 'it' was.

"I could not get close," Johannes said.

"But it exists?" The priest gave him a small shake as he spoke.

"I believe so, but there is no way to say for certain." Uncertainty crept into his voice. He doubted the priest would believe what he had seen. But then he remembered what was in the bag and why he had brought it. "If it is where I believe it is, death awaits anyone who ventures there."

The priest stood and folded his arms across his chest. "You will have to go back. I will send men with you to keep you safe."

"There aren't enough men to fight the devil himself!" Johannes was surprised at the strength in his own words. "His minions guard it."

The priest cocked his head. "Minions of the devil?"

"Monsters," Johannes croaked. "And I brought proof." With trembling hands, he opened the sack and upended it, spilling its contents onto the floor.

The priest sucked in his breath through gritted teeth and took a step back. "What are these foul things and why have you brought them into the house of God?"

"I needed to prove the truth of my words. It is just like the temple…"

"Are you mad?" the priest hissed. "You are in the cathedral. Remember yourself."

Johannes did remember, and he began to tremble as he recalled the past several days—the fight for his life and his desperate trek back to the cathedral, all the while fearing what might be following behind him. "The devil…" His mouth was suddenly dry. "The devil gathers all the light to himself. They will come for…" He raised an unsteady hand and pointed at the golden casket.

The priest seemed to understand immediately. He once again knelt alongside Johannes and placed a comforting hand on his shoulder. "I will do what needs to be done. You may rest now."

Johannes closed his eyes and let his shoulders sag. Rest would be a welcome thing.

His eyes snapped open as a fiery lance of pain tore through his chest. He tried to cry out, but his breath was gone. He looked down to see a knife hilt protruding from his chest.

"No, don't look at that. Look at me," the priest cooed.

Johannes looked into the amber eyes and saw nothing there. No compassion, no love, only emptiness.

"You have done well," the priest said. "The secrets must be kept. You understand."

"I… don't…" Johannes gasped.

The priest gave a sad smile, yanked the dagger free, and wiped it on Johannes' cloak. Gently, like a mother putting her babe to bed, he eased Johannes down onto the hard floor. The cold stone seemed to leach the remaining warmth from Johannes' body even as his life's blood flowed from the wound in his chest.

"You know much, yet you understand nothing."

The light seemed to dim around Johannes, and a circle of blackness slowly closed in on him. He watched as the priest gathered the contents of the sack, stepped over the altar, and moved to the golden casket. As death gathered him in its arms, Johannes whispered one final word.

"Dreihasenbild."

# CHAPTER 1

**This place was** cold– a biting, stinging, run home and put your feet up by the fire kind of cold that soaked through every layer of your clothing. Key West this was not.

"What are you thinking, Maddock?" Jade's sleek black hair was sprinkled with the powdery snow that floated down on the vagrant breeze. Her eyes sparkled with the reflected light of the lamp-lined street and her smile outshone the mantle of white that lay heavy on the world. "Don't tell me. You are so glad I talked you into this!"

Maddock grinned. He was glad he hadn't answered the question. He'd actually been wondering how Jade had extracted him from his well-worn holiday tradition of beer and barbecue somewhere, anywhere the only white thing blanketing the world was sand. Not wanting to spoil her good mood, he pulled her close and kept his thoughts to himself. They'd spent too much time apart of late. Jade had been working in the Far East while Maddock had been... too many places to count. She wanted this trip and this time together and he was happy to oblige her.

"Christmas in Germany!" she breathed. "I've dreamed about it ever since I was a little girl. The cathedrals! And..." she drew the word out like a game show host about to announce the grand prize "...the snow!" She swept out her arm, her gesture taking in the city's frosted skyline. "And then we're going to the Alps!" She squeezed him tight and bounced up and down like an excited child.

"Tell me again why we came here so early?" He enveloped her in his arms and they looked out across the Rhine River, the light of the street lamps flickering across its choppy surface.

"Because the celebration of the Christmas season started the evening of December sixth. I wanted to be here for more than just Christmas day! I've got tonight all planned out. We'll have our tour of the cathedral and then I've got a restaurant picked out where they serve some of the traditional holiday treats. "

"I hate fruitcake." He knew better, but it was worth it to see the scandalized look in her eyes, though it passed almost immediately.

"I am not letting you mess with me tonight. I'm too happy." She turned back toward the water. "And for your information, you are going to try Christbaumgeback even if it kills you." She glanced at her watch. "We should probably get going." Her face fell into a frown and she looked up and down the street.

Maddock's eyes followed hers, but he saw nothing amiss. "You never told me how you managed to schedule a solo, nighttime tour of the Cologne Cathedral."

"I know somebody," she kissed him on the left cheek, "who knows somebody," a kiss on the right cheek, "who knows somebody." The next kiss was full on the lips.

"Get a room you two!"

No way. It couldn't be who he thought it was. Jade was going to have a cow. Maddock turned to see a six-and-a-half foot tall Native American strolling along the river walk. His height and breadth of shoulder drew the attention of everyone he passed.

"You have got to be kidding me." Jade turned her angry eyes upon Maddock. "What is Bones doing here?"

Uriah Bonebrake, known to his friends as "Bones," was Maddocks business partner and best friend since their days as Navy SEALs. He also was not Jade's favorite person, nor was she his.

"I don't..." Maddock was dumbfounded. He'd only told Bones that he and Jade were going away for the holidays. How had Bones known where they were going, much less where they would be standing at this exact moment? "Bones, what the hell?"

"It's Christmas, dude!" Bones grinned. He wore his black leather biker jacket unzipped, revealing a t-shirt featuring a character from the South Park cartoon garbed in a Santa outfit with *Merry Bleeping Christmas* printed above the character's head. The fact that the shirt read "bleeping" instead of the actual expletive was unusually restrained for Bones. It wouldn't help with Jade's mood, though.

"I can't believe you invited Bones on our romantic Christmas getaway." If he'd thought the breeze coming across the river was frigid, Jade's words took it down a few degrees. "Is he sleeping in our bed too?"

"I..." Words failed him.

"You got punked!" Jade's icy expression melted into a warm smile. "I got you so bad, Maddock! I wish I had it on video."

"I got it." A female voice rang out and a young woman stepped out from the shadows a few paces away. "Maddock, you so got owned. Dude, your girlfriend rocks."

Angelica Bonebrake only vaguely resembled her brother. They both had long black hair and mischievous twinkles in their eyes, but that was where the similarities ended.

Where Bones' face was hard and chiseled, Angelica's features were soft and finely formed and, though she was tall for a woman, she was a far cry from her towering brother. She pocketed her camera and hurried forward to catch Maddock in a crushing embrace. She was beautiful, no doubt, but underneath her thick winter clothes she was one hundred forty pounds of solid muscle. When she wasn't working security at her uncle Crazy Charlie's casino, she was a bantamweight fighter in the WFFC. Many a drunken man had gotten too friendly with Angelica and had his shoulder dislocated or jaw broken for his trouble.

"I can't believe this." Maddock was almost dizzy with surprise. He turned to Jade, who beamed up at him. "You engineered this?"

"Did you really think I'd try to keep you away from your best friend at Christmas? It's a holiday for family and I know you guys always spend it together." The joy on her face made her even more beautiful.

He arched an eyebrow. "You're sure you want to spend Christmas with Bones?"

"Definitely." Jade turned to Angelica. "You must be Angelica. I'm Jade Ihara."

"You can just call me Angel."

Maddock cocked his head to the side. "When did this happen? I thought people called you Demonica."

"That was before she became a supermodel." Bones gave his sister a playful punch to the shoulder.

"I am not a model," she said through gritted teeth as she hit him back.

Bones rubbed his shoulder in mock hurt and Angel made an obscene gesture. "Hey chick, it's Christmas. Anyway," he turned to Maddock and Jade, "you are looking at the new female face of the WFFC!"

"It's no big deal." Angel looked embarrassed.

"She's on all their ads and she's got tons of endorsements." Bones clapped her on the back. "Of course, that might just be because all the other chicks are butt dog ugly."

Angel elbowed him in the gut and shoved him away. "I don't know why I agreed to come on this trip. You are such a..."

"Christmas!" Bones held up a hand, forestalling what Maddock was sure would have been one of Angel's streams of choice profanity. She could swear in English, Cherokee, Spanish and a smattering of several other languages.

"Don't listen to him," Jade said. "You're every bit as pretty as Maddock described you."

"Oh really?" Bones gave him an appraising look. "Now you're hot for my sister too? How many babes do you need?"

"What I said was, you must have gotten all the bad genes in the family."

"Don't hate," Bones said. "You've always been jealous of my good looks."

"How about we get going?" Jade said. "We're supposed to meet my friend at the cathedral in ten minutes."

A few minutes later found them rounding the Kölner Dom. The massive Gothic cathedral was, according to Jade, the largest in all of Germany. Maddock had never seen its equal. Its twin columns, square in their lower sections, octagonal in the middle and tapering off to points far above, were inlaid with stone reliefs and towered above them, almost sinister in the darkness.

"It withstood all the bombings during World War II." Jade spoke in a tone almost as soft as the downy flakes that fell harder as they approached the cathedral entrance. "Everything around it was leveled, but the cathedral stood."

Bones whistled, clearly impressed.

"Some think the Allies tried to avoid hitting it because its height made for a good landmark for pilots. Others credit more otherworldly protection." Her eyes flitted skyward for a moment before locking on a man who stood waving to them. He was tall and wiry with thinning brown hair sprinkled with white. He looked to be of late middle years, but his smile was eager and his eyes brimmed with vitality. He gave Jade a quick embrace before turning to introduce himself to the others.

"Otto Döring. I am an archaeologist and an old friend of Jade's." He had only the slightest German accent.

"Otto has pulled a few strings to get us access to the cathedral after regular tour hours." Jade beamed. "He is going to show us around."

Otto nodded and led the way through the main entrance, filling them in on details as they went. Bones snickered at the mention of "flying buttresses," but it turned to a wheezing cough when Angel elbowed him in the gut. Otto did not seem to notice, so absorbed was he in his subject. "The cathedral is nearly one hundred fifty meters long, more than eighty-five meters wide and over one hundred fifty meters high."

Maddock performed some quick calculations. That put the towers at over five hundred feet tall, the nave nearly that length, and the transept almost three-hundred feet wide. As they stepped inside, he fully appreciated the sheer size of the place and what it must have taken to construct it, considering the available technology between the thirteenth and nineteenth centuries. The towering columns drew his eyes up to the vaulted ceiling overhead. This place was an architectural marvel.

"The windows on the south wall were donated by ..." Otto's voice trailed away. "Oh my!" He pointed to the far end of the nave. "The Shrine of the Magi. What happened to it?"

"The what?"

"The Shrine of the Magi," Jade said. "The golden sarcophagus that supposedly holds the remains of the three Wise Men, who visited the baby Jesus."

Ignoring the others, Otto took off at a trot and Maddock ran alongside him as the archaeologist hurried toward the far end of the cathedral. They skirted the transept altar and ran toward the main altar.

Under a different set of circumstances, Maddock would have goggled at the ornate stained glass, the sculptures, and the artwork. Now, however, he had eyes only for the scene around the altar.

Three steps led up to the black marble altar outlined in ornate white friezes. Directly behind it stood the shattered remains of what had been a bulletproof glass container. Nearby lay an upended golden sarcophagus, and behind that were bodies.

# CHAPTER 2

Three men in clerical robes lay around the fallen sarcophagus as if they had tried to defend it from whoever was after it. Maddock knelt to check on the nearest man. He was dead. He'd been stabbed multiple times in the abdomen. Deep slices in his palms indicated defensive wounds. He glanced at Bones, who was examining another man. Bones shook his head.

"This man's alive." Angel knelt over the third man, feeling for a pulse. "But I don't think he has much time."

They surrounded the dying man, whose eyes suddenly popped open. He looked down at the blood soaking his vestments and he let his head fall back. He stared glassy-eyed at Angel, the knowledge of his certain death filling his eyes.

"Engel?" he gasped, reaching up to grab her by the sleeve.

"Angel, yes." She looked surprised. "How does he know my name?"

Considering the dying priest's probable delirium, Maddock thought, the beautiful young woman clad in a white jacket with a few snowflakes still dusting her hair probably looked like an actual angel to him. "I think he believes you're an actual angel." Maddock kept his voice low, as if they sat at a hospital bedside.

"You guys, look at that." Something had caught Jade's eye. Carefully skirting the fallen bodies, she moved closer to the fallen sarcophagus, which lay on its side like an upended house. The top had either fallen or been tossed to the side, and on the floor nearby lay three skulls and a scattering of bone fragments.

Jade slipped on her gloves and picked up one of the skulls to give it a closer look. Candlelight flickered across its surface, lending it a sinister feel.

"Do you think he's a Magi?" Maddock moved closer

to Jade, and Bones and Otto followed.

"I don't know what he is." Jade's voice trembled. "But he's not human." Slowly, as if turning over the last card in a losing hand, Jade rotated the skull for all to see.

Maddock stopped short. Behind him, he heard Bones' sharp intake of breath, and Otto's mumbled German curse. At least it sounded like a curse to Maddock.

Protruding from the skull were two small, curved horns.

"What the hell is that?" Maddock could not believe what he was seeing.

"Tuefel," Otto whispered, taking a step back.

The priest's eyes drifted toward Jade, and he seemed to experience a sudden moment of clarity as he saw what she was holding. "Nein!" he gasped. His grip on Angel's sleeve tightened and he rattled off a stream of words. He let go of her arm and pointed beyond the altar toward the apse, where seven chapels formed the cathedral's chevet. The priest was speaking so fast that Maddock could make out only a few words, though he did catch "Mailänder Madonna" and something that sounded like "dry house and build." He paused, gasping for breath, and hacked up a gout of blood. This seemed to take everything he had left. He let his head fall back and his eyes close. "Ewige." His voice was a scarce whisper. "Ewige." He coughed again. "L..." He fell silent as life fled his body.

"What did he say?" Angel's jaw was set and she looked like she was ready to punch anyone within arm's reach.

Otto held up a hand and shook his head. He took out a cell phone and made a call. His voice sounded both grave and urgent. When he finally hung up, he turned back to Angel. "I apologize. I felt I should call the authorities right away." He gave a quick shake of the head as if to jar his mind back on track. "The priest said the skulls must never be seen or people will lose faith. He begs us to take them away." Otto scratched his head.

"After that, I think he was confused. He said all the priests were dead and he had to share the secret or it could be lost forever."

"What secret was he talking about?" Bones asked.

"I do not know. As I said, he sounded confused, though he was insistent that I listen to him. I could see in his eyes that it was important." Otto looked around. "He mentioned the Milan Madonna, as you would say it in English, which is back there." He pointed to a statue that stood beyond the altar, far to the right, where the first chapel began. "It is a well-known work of art." Otto shrugged.

"He said something else," Maddock said. "It sounded like 'dry' something or other."

"Dreihasenbild. The three hares." When everyone looked puzzled, Otto continued. "The three hares is a symbol found on many churches, cathedrals, and other sites of religious significance, from England, all the way to the Far East. It depicts three hares chasing one another in a circle. The image is rendered in such a way that each hare has two ears, but there are only three ears in total in the image."

"I've heard of it," Jade said, "though it's not my area of expertise. It's a symbol of the Trinity, is it not?"

"It can be." Otto nodded. "But to the Pagans it can represent fertility or the moon cycle."

"How does fertility connect with the Madonna?" Angel rose to her feet, finally turning away from the priest.

"She got fertile after Jesus was born, didn't she?" Bones said.

"You're a pig." Angel scowled at her brother.

"No, really. I mean, he had brothers and sisters."

"That is true." Otto almost managed a smile. "In the middle ages, it was believed that the rabbit was a hermaphrodite that could reproduce without losing virginity, hence the connection to the Blessed Mother."

"I get it." Bones nodded. "So it's not an Easter Bunny thing." Everyone ignored him.

"Otto," Maddock began, "what was that last thing he said?"

"Ewige. It translates to English as *eternal, perpetual, everlasting.*"

"He didn't get the last word out." Angel folded her arms across her chest. "It started with an "l" though."

"What's the German word for life?" Bones asked.

"Leben."

"You mean like Chris Leben?" Angel grinned. "Chris Life doesn't really suit that guy." When Otto frowned, she shrugged. "Sorry. He and I are in the same line of work."

"If he was trying to say 'eternal life,' that would make sense, wouldn't it?" Bones asked. "He's a priest and this is a church."

"If I was dying," Angel added, "that would certainly be on my mind."

Otto shrugged. "I just cannot believe this. Why would someone kill these poor men, and why would they want the bones of the Magi?"

"Why would they bust open the sarcophagus and not take the bones?" Jade asked. "Unless these skulls were not what they expected to find."

"I do not think anyone expected to find skulls like...that." Otto took a deep breath and as he exhaled, seemed to deflate a little bit. "It is all too much. I do not understand why this has happened."

Maddock chewed on his lower lip. The gears in his mind were turning at a rapid clip. He had a sixth sense about secrets and mysteries, and something told him there was more to the priest's final words than mere confusion.

"As long as we've got to wait here until the police come, we might as well do a little searching. See if we can make sense of what the priest was saying."

"Great," Bones deadpanned. "Another Maddock mystery."

"I'm game." Angel headed straight for the Milan Madonna and looked it up and down. "What exactly should I be looking for?"

"Maybe the three rabbit thing?" Bones said, coming up to join her. "He did make a point to mention it."

Maddock turned and scanned the seven chapels. The priest had said "Mailänder Madonna" but he had pointed to the left side of the chevet– the side opposite the Madonna. He carefully stepped around the shattered bulletproof glass that lay scattered around the altar and moved into the chevet.

Each chapel was a recessed area containing works of art. He inspected them one by one, looking for... he didn't know what exactly. He thought Bones was on the right track in searching for the three hares. It was the sort of out-of-place symbol that might bear significance in a place like this.

His eyes were drawn to a large, busy painting. As he drew close, Otto joined him.

"*The Adoration of the Magi.* It depicts the donors being presented to the Madonna." He indicated the figures in the foreground. "In the back are shown scenes around the birth of the Christ child."

"The title is promising." On either side of the painting, a figure knelt before a draped table, and on each drape a symbol was rendered– a dark background with three shapes. His heart racing, Maddock moved closer but was disappointed to find that the symbols were fleur-de-lis, not hares. He took hold of the frame and pulled, but it did not budge. He gave it a push, which made no difference either.

Jade sidled up to him and peered at the painting with keen interest. "You think there's something here, Maddock?"

"I don't know. Just checking it out." He ignored the foreground for the moment and examined the background images. The world swam in his peripheral vision, and he was about to give up when something caught his eye. "Otto, what is this scene?"

"That is the Christ Child being presented in the temple."

He could clearly make out the scene in the temple, but the artist had slipped some odd images into the scene: a child performing a handstand, a flock of birds, and animal that could have been a cat, or perhaps a rabbit, and..."

"What is this here?" He indicated a brown triskelion-like shape in front of one of the temple columns.

Otto leaned in close and his eyes widened with surprise when they fell on the spot Maddock indicated. "Ja! I think it might be the three hares!"

Maddock wasted no time. He placed his thumb over the image, grimacing at the thought of damaging the work of art. He pressed down gently. There was definitely something underneath, a raised bump or... a button. Before he could change his mind, he pressed down hard.

He felt the raised area give way, heard a click, and a loud scraping sound filled the silent cathedral. He sprang back, putting his arms out to shield Jade and Otto, but there was no need. The portion of the wall where the painting hung slid forward. Maddock stepped around behind it and saw a hole in the floor just big enough for a person to enter. There was no ladder, but he could see handholds cut into the stone.

"Sweet!" Bones was leaning over his shoulder, looking down at the passageway Maddock had discovered. "Me first!"

Otto gaped at the discovery. "I cannot believe this." He gave a sad smile. "It seems I am saying that a great deal this evening." He straightened and looked Maddock in the eye. "Clearly the priest was not confused. There is a mystery here, though I cannot imagine what it is all about." He turned to Jade. "There could be much at stake here, and if there is a secret, it should be entrusted to someone who understands the value of history and of spirituality." He held out his hand. "I trust you."

They shook hands and exchanged a solemn look.

"Go now. Die Polizei should be here soon. I am a regular visitor here so my presence will not rouse suspicion. Perhaps we can keep you and this mystery out of the public eye until you can uncover the truth."

They thanked Otto and, one by one, climbed down into the darkness. Bones led the way and Maddock brought up the rear. As he descended into the shaft, he saw Otto wave goodbye and reach up to press the button on the painting. The section of wall slid back into place, plunging them into darkness.

# CHAPTER 3

**Maddock took it** slow, careful not to rush Jade and Angel who were not experienced climbers. A faint light blossomed down below. Bones held his latest favorite gadget—a combination ink pen, flashlight, and laser pointer that he frequently used to entertain cats and annoy everyone else. When he reached the bottom, he fished his own keychain flashlight out of his pocket and he and Bones shone their lights all around.

They were in a circular chamber, the stones fitted neatly together with expert craftsmanship. He saw no doorways, trapdoors, or anything that would indicate a means of egress.

"Dead end?" Angel looked around. "I sure don't see anything here."

"Places like this are never as they seem." Maddock hoped he wasn't about to be made to look the fool. "The sign of the three hares is what got us down here, so I'd guess we're looking for something similar."

"You mean like what's right next to your foot?" Jade too had taken out a small flashlight and directed the beam down at the floor where Maddock stood. A manhole-sized disc carved with the three hare symbol was set in the floor.

"Why am I the only one with no flashlight?" Angel stood with her arms folded. "It's not exactly an essential, yet you all have one?"

"We're archaeologists," Jade explained as she and Maddock knelt down to give the disc a closer examination. "You never know when you're going to find yourself crawling into a cave or a dark tunnel." She held her flashlight in her teeth, grasped the disc with both hands, and tugged. It did not budge.

"Maybe it turns. Let's get some extra muscle on it." Maddock found handholds on the raised portion of the carving and was surprised when Angel lent a hand.

"You want muscle? You want me, not Bones. He's a wuss." She flashed her brother an evil grin. He, in turn, flashed her an obscene gesture, which only elicited a laugh. "On three?"

Maddock counted to three and they heaved. The stone circle held fast for a moment, then gave way so suddenly that Maddock almost fell on his face. They continued rotating the stone until it came free, then slid it aside. Damp, musty air, warmed by the earth far below the frozen streets, rose up to meet them. It was a short drop to a narrow passageway down below.

Angel looked at him with questioning eyes.

"In for a penny, in for a pound." Maddock pocketed his light, dropped down into the tunnel, and stepped out of the way. The others followed in short order.

The passage in which they found themselves was scarcely wide enough for two people to walk abreast, and the ceiling was so low that it barely cleared the top of Bones' head. It ran only about ten paces in each direction, each end terminating at a stone door flanked by Doric columns and surmounted by a Roman-style arch.

"So, do we take a left turn at Albuquerque?" Bones flicked his light back and forth, examining each door in turn. "Of course, I don't see any rabbits in here."

The figures of five women were carved in each door. The women on the left held containers and gazed out with expectant expressions on their faces. Maddock marveled at the skill of the sculptor whose stonework could convey such emotion. The women in the carving to the right averted their faces, some looking down, and one even covering her face with the hem of her cloak.

"Weird." Maddock mulled their options. "I know which door I'm inclined to stay away from." He indicated the women with downcast and averted faces, "But I'd like something more solid to go on."

Jade narrowed her eyes and looked like she was about to say something when Angel chimed in.

"I know this story. These are the ten virgins!" She smiled and punched Bones in the shoulder. "Dude! I remember it from vacation Bible school when we were kids."

"I was going to say the same thing," Jade agreed. "Not my specialty, but I felt pretty sure. Angel just confirmed it."

"Ten virgins. Nice." Bones grinned and danced out of the way before Angel could punch him again.

"So what's the story?" It sounded familiar to Maddock, but that was about it.

"It's a parable, also known as the Wise and Foolish Virgins. Ten virgins waited late into the night for the bridegroom to arrive. The foolish virgins," Jade pointed to the door on the right, "were unprepared and had no oil for their lamps. They are left out of the marriage feast. The wise virgins were prepared, so they were rewarded. It's supposed to be a lesson to always be ready for the second coming. To always keep the light burning, so to speak."

"Wise Virgins," Maddock looked to the door on the left, "and Wise Men." He looked upward. "Can't be a coincidence."

"Let's do it." Bones strode to the door.

"Wait up!" Angel said, hurrying after him. "You guys have done crap like this before. I've never gotten to open a big, scary door."

Bones stepped aside. "Be my guest." He motioned with both hands, doorman-style, and shook his head like a bemused parent as she brushed past him.

What had looked like a single door was actually two. A fine line ran up the center, and an iron ring was set on each side. "Here we go. One for each of us." Angel grabbed hold of one of the rings and indicated Bones should take the other. They heaved in unison, and the doors swung outward on unseen hinges. The space behind was pitch black. Angel put a hand out, as if the darkness itself had substance.

"Somebody with a flashlight can go first."

Chuckling, Bones led the way. They entered a room twenty paces long and ten across. Columns lined the walls and arches rose up to support the vaulted ceiling. An altar of white marble stood in the center of the room. At the far end, the figure of a nude man was carved into the wall. He held a cup in one hand and an ivy-wrapped staff in the other, and leaned against a stump wrapped in grape vines with bunches of grapes hanging from the top.

"Dionysus." Bones said. "God of wine and hard-partying. That's the man right there!"

"Bacchus, actually." Jade shone her light on the figure. "He's the Roman version of Dionysus. Subtle differences but, in essence, the same."

"A temple to one of the old Roman gods down here underneath one of the best-known cathedrals in the world?" Maddock shook his head. "This is crazy."

"Maybe not. The Romans came here in 50 AD, long before Christianity took hold in their empire. There are plenty of Roman ruins in, and even under, Cologne. I'll wager this place pre-dates the cathedral." Jade played her light around the temple. "It's interesting that the way down here was preserved and that someone along the way didn't destroy it. You'd think the church would consider this place blasphemous."

Maddock mulled that over as he approached the altar. The darkness in the room had hidden what lay atop it. It was a black figure of vaguely human shape. His first, terrible thought was of a badly burnt child, but when the beam of his light fell upon the crowned head, he knew it was something else entirely.

"Jade, do you see what I see?"

"It's the Milan Madonna!" Jade hurried to the altar and leaned down for a closer look. She glanced up at the confused faces all around her. "The Madonna upstairs is actually the second one. The old cathedral was destroyed by fire in 1248, and it was thought the original Madonna was destroyed as well, but apparently not, because here she is."

"The priest must have wanted us to find her, but why?" Maddock looked down at the blackened figure. Only the head was recognizable. The rest merely a scorched remnant of what had once been a classic work of art.

"I've got a crazy idea." Bones moved around the altar and stood at the Madonna's head. "You've got the three kings. Kings wear crowns." With that, he placed a hand on the statue's head, grasped the crown in the other, and twisted.

Maddock winced, wondering if his friend was going to destroy a piece of history, but the crown came free in his hand.

"It's hollow." Jade reached inside and withdrew a stone disc about the width of a man's hand. She held it up and shone her light on it. The three hares were carved on one side, and tiny writing was engraved in an ever-tightening spiral on the back. "It's German," she whispered, "an old form. We'll need someone to translate this for us."

Everyone jumped as the silence was broken by the sound of stone sliding on stone and a loud crash reverberated through the temple as the doors swung closed. Maddock and Bones hurried over and pushed against them, but the doors did not budge. Jade and Angel joined them, and they searched for a release lever, but to no avail. They were trapped.

# CHAPTER 4

**Niklas looked both** ways before exiting the treasury. It had been a frustrating search. The American, who had been put in charge of this mission, had said that they were looking for "instructions" and that he would know it when he found it. The man's face had contorted with rage when they had opened the Shrine of the Three Kings and found only those strange skulls. Of course, the man's scarred face, partly hidden by the wraparound sunglasses he wore day and night, always looked like it was twisted into a scowl.

The priests had been of no use. They had tortured them one by one and hadn't gotten a thing out of them. The ensuing search, thorough but careful, had proved equally fruitless. Niklas exchanged nervous glances with Ulrich as they stood in the snow and waited for their leader to give them further instructions.

The American was a bear of a man with a personality to match. Despite his battered body and pronounced limp, he moved with a confident, deadly air, like a caged beast ready to be unleashed at any moment. Niklas had seen him lose control only once, and it was not a sight he wanted to ever witness again.

"I think we're done here." The voice was a low growl. "I've changed my mind about those freak skulls. We'll take them with us. They must be a clue though I can't see how."

Privately, Niklas thought they should have taken the skulls with them in the first place, but the scarred man's rage had been so overwhelming that he had refused to even look at them, and neither Niklas nor Ulrich was about to argue with him. At least he had changed his mind. At worst, they would have something to show their superiors.

They slipped back inside the cathedral, the warm air

a welcome after the chilly winter breeze. Niklas moved silently, more out of habit than necessity. It was after hours and they had dispatched the few living men inside the Kölner Dom. There was no danger.

They rounded the corner of the transept, turned toward the nave, and froze. A man sat on the floor alongside the dead priests. His face was buried in his hands and he was speaking softly, the rhythm of his words indicating he was at prayer.

The American held a finger to his lips. He motioned for Ulrich to keep watch at the main entrance and for Niklas to follow him. He moved like a shadow across the floor, impressive considering his bulk and awkward gait. He was on the praying man in an instant, wrapping his thick arm around the man's throat like a python squeezing its prey, and lifting him up off the ground. The man kicked, flailed, and made squelching noises, but froze when the American spoke.

"You answer my questions, you might live."

That was surely a lie, but it wasn't Niklas' problem.

"You try anything at all and you die. Painfully. Understand?"

The man nodded. He kept his eyes squeezed shut, as if he could deny what was happening.

The American sat him down and the man dropped to his knees. He was shaking so hard he could barely remain upright.

"Tell me what you know."

"I... I know nothing. I come here to study..."

*Snap!* The American broke the man's little finger eliciting a shriek of agony.

"Shut up and listen." His tone was enough to cut off their prisoner's screams. "I can tell when you're lying. I can tell when you leave things out. And I... don't... care... how much I hurt you. I'll cut your eyeballs out and eat a damn Big Mac while I do it. You got me?"

Niklas' limited knowledge of American cuisine did not include 'damn Big Mac' but the words seemed to do the job. He saw the paltry bit of resistance drain from the man as his shoulders sagged and his chin fell to his chest.

Torture was something only an exceptional person could endure for any length of time. He had faced his share as part of his training prior to induction into the Heilig Herrschaft. Maintaining one's focus on the Most Holy was central to the denial of pain. Academics like the man who cowered before them usually broke quickly, for they had faith in nothing.

"Tell me everything."

The prisoner nodded vigorously and launched into an explanation, his words coming in short, disjointed bursts as if each phrase was trying to jostle the others out of the way so it could be heard first.

"One priest was not dead. He made no sense. He said he had a secret. Mailänder Madonna. Dreihasenbild. He made no sense."

"That can't be everything." The American reached for the knife at his waist, but the prisoner kept talking.

"He tried to say something else, but he died. All he said was 'ewige' and then he died." The prisoner stiffened as if waiting for something to happen. Indeed, Niklas expected the American to kill the man soon, if not now. "It is true. I swear it!" The man's eyes remained firmly shut. This might be a bad dream, but it was one from which he would not wake.

The American looked around and froze.

"Where are the skulls?" His voice was velvet soft, and it sent frozen fingers like the touch of a spirit down Niklas' spine.

The man hesitated and, for a moment, Niklas thought the fellow might try to hold something back, but courage apparently failed him.

"The others took them. I was giving them a tour, and they took the skulls."

"Did they hear the priest's words?" Heat rose in the American's voice.

"Yes. They hear everything. Then they took the skulls and left. I stayed here to wait for die Polizei."

So the authorities were on their way. That changed

things. Niklas looked around as if uniformed men lurked in the shadows.

"I want names, and fast."

"I do not know them all. They introduced themselves quickly and then we saw the priests." The man was shaking; clearly fearing this lack of knowledge would cost him his life. "One man was a red Indian. A big man, almost two meters tall. There was a woman, also a red Indian. I do not remember their names. And there was another man and woman."

"You'd better come up with at least one name or the remainder of your very short life will be filled with pain."

"Verzeih mir," the man whispered. *Forgive me.* "Jade Ihara. She was a colleague..."

"Jade Ihara the archaeologist?"

"Ja." The man nodded, his body quaking.

"They are here!" Ulrich called. "They did not use their sirens. We have no time."

The American let out roar of rage and frustration and clubbed the prisoner across the temple, knocking him unconscious.

The three men dashed back to the transept and slipped outside, past the treasury, and across the street. Ten minutes later they were in their vehicle, driving along the Rhine. The American sat in the passenger side, muttering to himself. Niklas finally broke the silence.

"This Jade Ihara, you know her?" He bit his lip, waiting for the explosion, but it did not come.

"Oh yes. I know her well, and if I don't miss my guess, I know the men she's with. But they think I'm dead."

# CHAPTER 5

"You have got to be kidding me." Angel's tone was as flat as her stare as she stepped back and regarded the closed door. "I thought you guys were winding me up when you told me about your crazy adventures."

"I wish." Maddock shone his light on the door and ran his fingers along its surface, but felt no switch or lever. "The good news is, there's always a way out."

"How can you be sure?" Angel didn't sound doubtful– only curious.

"You see any remains in here? Obviously, everyone who came in here left again. We just need to figure out how." He continued to search. "Let's start by looking for either the sign of the three hares or the wise virgins. This is a pagan temple, so I think the hares are more likely."

They spread out and continued the search. It wasn't long before Jade called everyone over to the Bacchus frieze.

"I found the hares!" She shone her light over a bunch of grapes.

Maddock and the others circled around behind her and looked where she indicated. He frowned.

"I don't see anything but grapes."

"You won't at first. Step back and squint." Jade turned and flashed a bright smile. "Tilt your head if you have to."

They must have made an odd-looking trio, the three of them leaning to and fro, looking from different angles, trying to see what Jade saw. She moved the side and shone her light across the carving, casting it in long shadows.

"There it is!" Bones' voice was triumphant. "It's like one of those weird posters where you have to let your vision go all fuzzy before you can see it."

Almost as soon as Bones had spoken, Maddock saw

it too. It wasn't quite a stereogram, but some of the grapes were raised far above the others, and when seen in the proper light, the image swam into focus, forming a shape that resembled the three hares.

"Give it a push." Maddock held his breath as Jade pressed her palm to the carving. He saw no seam that would indicate that the hare sign was anything other than a clever artistic detail, but after a moment, Jade's hand slowly moved forward as the hares slid into the wall. Something snapped into place and the wall sank slowly into the floor, revealing an upward-sloping passageway, the twin of the one that had brought them here.

The way was long and steep, but uneventful. They finally came to a blank wall. The ceiling here was low, and even Jade had to duck to avoid banging her head. Maddock shone his light on the ceiling. There were no hares or wise virgins here, only two handholds set in a square stone as wide as his shoulders. He reached for it and hesitated. What, or who, would they find on the other side?

"Do you think we're back at the cathedral?" Angel asked.

"No. This tunnel was almost a straight shot moving away from the cathedral. I think we're closer to the river." The air was cooler here and, he thought, just a touch more humid.

"Does it really matter?" Bones stared up at the trapdoor as he spoke. "It's not like there's anywhere else to go."

"True." Maddock nodded. "Tell you what. If we wind up in the middle of someone's living room, you and Angel start talking in Cherokee and Jade can chime in with Japanese. Act confused and get the hell out of there."

"What about you?" Bones eyed him, an amused smile on his lips. "What other language do you speak, Maddock?"

Maddock grinned. He knew a smattering of German

and French, and enough Spanish to order drinks and a meal and to ask for directions to the bathroom, but none of those would help. "Pig Latin."

Bones chuckled as the two of them pushed up on the trapdoor. They lifted it up and set it over to the side. Up above, faint yellow light flickered on an arched stone roof.

"Another cathedral," Maddock muttered. He helped the others up and then climbed out with an assist from Bones. Looking around, he knew immediately he had been correct. This was not the Kölner Dom. The interior, though impressive in its architecture, was austere. It lacked Kölner Dom's splendor, the stained glass one of the few sources of color.

"This is St. Martin's," Jade whispered. "It was almost destroyed in World War II and rebuilt afterward."

"You can tell us all about it later." Maddock slid the stone back into place, took Jade's hand, and led the way out.

Just before they reached the doors leading out, a white-robed man appeared. He spotted Maddock, frowned, and opened his mouth to speak. And then he spotted Bones. As was often the case, the sight of the massive Cherokee rendered him speechless. He gaped as Bones took out his wallet, withdrew a twenty, and pressed it into the monk's hand.

"A da ne di." Bones smiled, patted the monk on the shoulder, and led the way out.

"What did you say to him?" Jade asked.

"I told him, in Cherokee, to get himself a happy ending massage."

"He's lying." Angel seemed to have given up punching her brother, and gave him a dirty look instead. "He told him it was a gift."

"It was either that or punch the dude. I figured he has enough problems already. You know, no cash, boring clothes, no babes."

Maddock had to laugh. "Remind me about this next time I complain about your ugly mug."

"Right." Bones feigned disbelief. "Everybody knows I'm the good-looking one."

# CHAPTER 6

**The winter garden** in Heller's Brauhaus was decked out for the holiday season. Traditional music played in the background, scarcely audible over the talk and laughter in the crowded pub. The cheerful atmosphere was at odds with Maddock's gray mood which had only begun to lighten when Jade had received a text from Otto letting them know he was all right and had been released after being questioned by the police. They had sampled a few German Christmas specialties and were digging into plates of Braumeisterbraten, a pork roast in beer sauce, and drinking Kolsch, a local specialty beer, when Otto wandered in with a bandage on his finger and looking dazed but otherwise whole. He declined Maddock's offer to buy his dinner, but accepted a Kolsch and drank half of it in three large gulps.

"I don't feel right about leaving you there by yourself," Maddock told him. "We should have stayed with you." The others agreed. Excited as they were about the discovery they had made, leaving the man to face the authorities alone felt wrong.

"No, no." Otto waved away their apologies. "The police would have taken the skulls and we would not have had a chance to look for the hidden passage. The place is now a crime scene. There is no telling how long it will be before it is once again open to the public." He took another swallow of his beer, this one moderate, and wiped his mouth on his shirt sleeve before continuing. "I also agree with the priest. If the public knew the Shrine of the Magi held such grotesqueries..." He pinched his lower lip, his eyes narrowed in thought.

"What do you think they are?" Angel asked. "Have you ever seen anything like them?"

"Never. I suspect they are forgeries– a sinister joke left behind by whoever stole the real skulls of the Magi."

"So you think the bones of the Wise Men really were in the shrine at some point in the past?" Maddock had been wondering if perhaps the horned skulls had been there from the beginning.

"If the records are to be believed, the shrine once contained three crowned skulls. This was supposedly verified by priests at Kölner Dom. Of course, everything is in question now." Otto lapsed back into deep thought, then his eyes suddenly brightened and he looked at Jade. "Where are the skulls now?"

"Back in our hotel room. I thought about leaving them in the temple, but changed my mind."

"What temple?" Otto's eyes shone with disbelief as they filled him in on what lay beneath Kölner Dom.

"A temple to a Roman god beneath Cologne's most sacred site. It is difficult to accept. Of course, ours is a tangled history." He smiled sadly. "Why do you suppose the priest wanted someone to know about it? Would it not have been best for the church to let it fall from memory? If he was the keeper of the secret, he need not have passed it along."

"Jade left out the most interesting part." Maddock smiled. "She does that for dramatic effect."

"I was getting there, Maddock." She blushed, giving her almond-colored skin a warm, pleasant hue. "But you go ahead."

"You've got the disc. You tell the story." Maddock took a long pull of his Kolsch, savoring its sweet, almost fruity flavor, something between ale and lager. He glanced at Otto, whose eyes sparkled as he leaned in close, his beer forgotten as he waited for the rest of the story. Bones smirked and Angel grinned behind her glass.

"But you're the one who found the compartment inside the Milan Madonna." Jade played along. "You should tell him."

"Disc? Milan Madonna?" Otto sounded like a little boy, early on Christmas morning, begging to open his gifts.

They all took long pulls of Kolsch, prolonging the moment as Otto's pleading eyes darted around the table, eager for someone to let him in on the secret.

"It was nothing much," Jade said, placing her glass on the table and reaching into her purse. "We found the original Milan Madonna and this was hidden inside of her." She handed Otto an object wrapped in a handkerchief.

He held it gingerly and unwrapped it with care, holding it close to his chest and hunching over as if to hide it from prying eyes. Maddock thought the man need not bother. The place was packed, mostly with young people overindulging in ale and holiday cheer, and no one was paying them a bit of attention.

When Otto's eyes fell on the three hares, he gaped. He turned it in his hands, gazing at the ancient symbol. Apparently satisfied there was nothing more to see there, he turned it over. "Latin?" he asked as he once again turned the disc, his eyes following the writing that spiraled in toward the center.

"That's what we thought." Jade sounded annoyed. "But nothing translates, at least not on any of the websites I tried." She shrugged and made an apologetic face. "My specialty is the native tribes of the southwestern United States, and I've branched out into eastern Asia. My knowledge of this part of the world is comparatively small."

"I think," Otto said, a ghost of a grin materializing on his face, "that it is Latin, but in a cipher."

Now it was Maddock's turn to grin. He had suspected the same thing and had sent photographs of the disc to his friend Jimmy Letson, an accomplished hacker and a computer whiz of the first order. Jimmy had replied with a text that read, *I do have a life, you know,* but if Maddock knew Jimmy, he was already hard at work cracking the code. Like Maddock and Bones, the man relished a challenge, though his specialty was of the cyber realm rather than the archaeological.

"Any idea what kind of cipher it might be?"

Maddock asked Otto, who was fixated on the text.

"I cannot say at first glance," he mumbled. "The Caesar shift cipher was commonly used in the church. One simply chooses a number to shift the letters, either to the right or to the left. A shift of one to the right and the letter 'A' becomes 'B' and so on. It is simple enough for a priest who was not a cryptographer to use, but complicated enough to fool the average person."

"Could the average person even read back then?" Angel asked.

"We do not, of course, know the time period when this cipher was written, if that is indeed what it is. If it is more than a few centuries old, you are certainly correct, particularly for a message in Latin."

"Any chance it's a fake?" Angel asked.

Otto tilted his hand back-and-forth. "It is possible, but the temple and the Madonna suggest otherwise."

Maddock nodded. It was the same conclusion they had drawn. He was looking around for a server from whom to order another round of Kolsch when his cell phone vibrated in his pocket. It was Jimmy.

*"Why don't you give me something that requires neurons next time, like a ten-piece kindergarten puzzle?"*

"I take it you've deciphered our cipher." At those words, all eyes at the table turned to Maddock.

*"If you can call it that."* Jimmy was clearly disappointed at the lack of challenge posed by the text on the disc. *"It was one of the most common ciphers ever."*

"The Caesar shift?" Maddock asked. Relishing Jimmy's sudden silence, he caught the eye of an attractive blonde waitress and signaled for five more drinks. She nodded and gave him a wink that did not escape Jade's notice. She arched an eyebrow at him, but then smiled.

*"You're smarter than you look, Maddock,"* Jimmy finally said, sounding even more disappointed. *"Want to take a guess at the key?"*

"The what?"

*"The number of the shift. How many letters over you*

*count when substituting the new letter."* A bit of Jimmy's cockiness was returning.

Maddock thought immediately of the Wise Men. "Three."

*"All right, Carnac, which direction?"*

Maddock decided not to spoil all of Jimmy's fun. "No idea."

*"The right. You should have known that. This is more of that ancient church crap. Right hand of God. Left hand is unclean..."*

"True. I'm a little distracted right now. I'm sitting in a pub in Cologne, downing a few brews with a couple of beautiful women."

*"You're such an ass, Maddock."* Jimmy chuckled. *"Of course, Bones is probably there too, which sucks all the fun out of everything."*

"I'll tell him you said so. Can you send me the translation?"

*"Sure. The last word was partially rubbed out or chipped away or something, so I didn't get it all. Emailing it to you right now. And, of course, you owe me a meal... again."*

"What would I ever do without you? Thanks, Jimmy."

Maddock ended the call and punched up his email on his phone. Everyone leaned toward him as he began to read.

*"As the lion roars for the king, the peacock be your guide into the depths of the well. The kings point the way to the falling ice that hides eternal l..."*

It ended just as Jimmy had said– with an incomplete word.

"There it is again," Bones said. "You know, we figured the priest just didn't manage to get the last word out, but if he knew the words on this disc, maybe he was trying to tell us all he knew."

"Maybe." Maddock looked up as their next round of

drinks arrived. He found he had lost his thirst, though, and drank mechanically as he pondered the words. "It's a far cry from step-by-step instructions."

"And this should lead us to the missing skulls, you think?" Jade leaned over to read Jimmy's email. She shook her head. "The wording makes it sound like there's something more. But what?"

"Should we go to the police with this?" Angel asked.

"I don't know." Bones spoke slowly, absently spinning his beer mug as he thought the problem through. "What do we really know? The killers want the skulls of the wise dudes. I'm guessing you told them as much." He looked at Otto who nodded. "We could give them this clue but what would they do with it? Can you see a cop who's probably got a ton of cases on his hands taking the time to trying to figure this thing out? That's what *we* do."

"I could share this with the police," Otto volunteered. "I will tell them it is something I found in my research. I suspect it will all be meaningless to them, but at least we will not be holding back anything significant." He frowned as he said the last.

Maddock nodded. It made sense. Still the fact that they were hiding their presence at a murder scene, though they arrived after the fact, felt wrong. He remembered that the killers had left no footprints, and he had a hunch they'd been careful not to leave behind any fingerprints or DNA.

"The safest course would be to go on with our vacation and just forget the whole thing. Then again, my gut tells me the only hope there is for finding the murderers lies with us. Maybe if we can solve this riddle we can figure out who was after the Magi's bones and why. Even then, who knows what we can really prove?"

"I say we go for it." Bones had the familiar gleam in his eyes that Maddock associated with the start of a treasure hunt. "What better way to celebrate Christmas than solve the mystery of the lost bones of the Magi?"

Jade nodded. "You know I'm in. And you," she

turned to Maddock, "live for this stuff, whether you want to admit it or not."

Maddock grinned. He and Jade were kindred spirits; both loved the sea, archaeology, and mysteries. That left only one person. He turned to Angel, whose cheeks were aglow and her brown eyes sparkling as she gazed back at him. He was suddenly struck by her beauty, and there was something in her expression that made him uneasy. He was pleased to see that Jade's attention was once again on the stone disc, and she hadn't seen whatever might have passed across his face. He took a quick drink, buying himself a moment to clear his head.

"How about you, Angel? You signed up for a vacation, not a mystery."

"Are you stupid? I'm all over it. Do you know how sick I am of Bones coming home and bragging about wrestling Bigfoot and all the other crap you two get up to?" Her roguish grin was so like that of her brother that it made Maddock flinch. It was one thing to notice Angel was hot. To think that *Bones' sister* was hot– that was something else entirely.

Otto cleared his throat.

"There is something else I must tell you." Not meeting anyone's eye, Otto recounted the time after they had left him alone in the cathedral. His voice was soft, remorse weighing heavily in every word. "I told them about the three hares." He lapsed into silence, but Maddock sensed there was more. "And I gave them Jade's name."

Maddock and Jade exchanged glances. He couldn't tell exactly what she was thinking, but she didn't seem too upset about it. She was tough.

"One of them knew you and he sounded very upset when I told him your name." Now Jade did look surprised, but she kept her silence. "That was when the authorities arrived." Otto finally looked at her. "I am so sorry. I have read adventure novels and imagined myself a hero, but reality is something entirely different. I am not a strong man." His chin fell to his chest and his face darkened.

"It's all right." Jade took his hand in both of hers. "I would have done the same thing."

Maddock knew that wasn't true. Jade was stronger than Otto ever dreamed of being.

"This is really jacked-up," Bones said to Jade. "If you have any rivals in your field, they would have one of your specializations, wouldn't they?"

Jade shrugged. "I suppose."

Maddock looked at Bones and could tell they were thinking the same thing. There was only one group that was likely to have it in for Jade. If his hunch was correct, they were all in danger.

# CHAPTER 7

"Did he say what, exactly, we are looking for?" Ulrich appeared in the doorway looking annoyed. "I searched the other two rooms and found nothing but suitcases that had not even been opened. It appears Ihara's friends checked in and stayed only long enough to drop off their luggage." He ran his fingers through his wavy black hair. His vanity and legendary poor swimming ability had earned him the nickname Hasselhoff, though few dared say it to the quick-tempered man's face.

"The skulls, obviously, and anything else that might connect to the three hares, the Magi, or the cathedral." Niklas finished his search of the bag. Neither it nor Ihara's luggage had turned up anything. The name on the identification tag read Dane Maddock. The name meant nothing to him, but he committed it to memory all the same.

"Have you found anything?" Ulrich opened the bathroom door and peered inside.

"I have not yet finished." Niklas felt a flash of annoyance. He did not want to leave empty-handed, but he was concerned that Ihara had taken the skulls with her. He searched the dresser, closet, and even the floor beneath the bed skirt, but came up empty. Ulrich poked around, looking in all the places Niklas had already checked.

He was about to give up when he noticed a bulge behind the curtain. Not wanting to give away his presence to anyone looking in from the outside, he drew back the curtain just far enough to see a black backpack resting on the windowsill. Dark, hollow holes gaped up at him from sinister, horned skulls. He had found what they were looking for.

"I've got them! Let's go."

Ulrich's tense face sagged with relief. He cracked the

door open and peered up and down the hall before signaling that the way was clear.

They took the stairs down to the first floor and, along the way, Niklas slipped out of his overcoat and draped it over his arm, concealing the backpack. Neither Ihara nor the rest of her party knew him or Ulrich, but there was always the slim chance she would recognize her own backpack, and he did not want to risk blowing things through a chance encounter. By the time they exchanged the warmth of the hotel for the cold December night, he knew he had made the right choice.

Four people approached, talking and laughing. Though he had never seen a picture of Ihara, he knew this had to be her. An attractive young woman of mixed Asian ancestry along with two American natives– one a tall, muscular man with long hair and a roguish face, the other an attractive twenty-something girl with captivating eyes. How many of their race did one see in Cologne? The fourth member of their group was a muscular man with blond hair and eyes the color of a stormy sea. This must be Dane Maddock. Though he smiled and spoke with his friends, his eyes locked on Niklas and Ulrich as if he somehow knew something was amiss with them. Then again, perhaps it was because Niklas was not wearing his coat despite the snowfall that was growing heavier by the minute.

They passed close enough for him to catch a whiff of Ihara's jasmine-scented perfume, and to realize just how tall the Indian was. Niklas was six feet tall, a shade taller than Maddock, but the Indian had him by at least half a head. Tension climbed his spine, knotting the muscles in his back and neck. He had a bad feeling about these two men and, though he and Ulrich were armed, he would prefer not to have an encounter with them.

By the time they reached their car, the group was rounding the corner of the hotel. He breathed a sigh of relief, set the backpack containing the skulls in the back, and slid into the driver's seat. He looked at Ulrich, who was standing on the sidewalk staring back at the hotel.

He called his name, but Ulrich raised a hand.

"Wait a moment. I will be right back." With that, he vanished into the swirling cloud of white.

**Angel pulled up** her hood, lowered her head against the wind and snow, and hurried along the sidewalk. How dumb had she been to leave her purse in the rental car? She wasn't a girly girl by any measure, but her wallet, passport, and phone were inside it and she didn't want to risk it getting stolen.

She was in such a hurry that she didn't notice the man approaching her until he was almost on top of her. They had just passed one another moments before. Great! Another random stranger hitting on her. She pushed back her hood and turned, about to deflect his advances with a polite rejection when he reached out, grabbed hold of her French braid, and yanked her forward.

"Come quietly and you will not..."

His words ended in a grunt as Angel drove a fist into his gut. The average person would have instinctively tried to pull away from the attacker and get loose from his grip, but Angel was not an average person. Her fighting instincts kicking in, she drove the heel of her palm up into her attacker's chin. He turned at the last instant and her strike caught him on the jaw. He took a step back, trying to yank her off balance by her hair. Angel barely noticed the pain; she'd had much worse in the octagon. As he moved backward, she scooped one of his legs and drove him backward. He was bigger than she was, and maybe stronger, but her aggressiveness caught him completely off guard. He stumbled back against a parked car, letting go of her hair as he fell hard to the ground. She heard the whoosh of breath leaving his lungs and the satisfying *thunk* as the back of his head cracked the sidewalk. The snow had probably cushioned the impact a little, but not much.

"Don't you know," Angel growled as she pummeled his face with sharp blows, "boys aren't supposed to fight girls? It's not gentlemanly."

The man flailed about weakly, trying to fight her off and regain his breath at the same time. She should probably get away while he was still too stunned to chase her, but she wasn't known for making good decisions when angry. He caught hold of the front of her coat with one hand and pulled her toward him. She used the added momentum to her advantage, driving her elbow into the bridge of his nose. Her coat was thick, but the padding was not enough to save his nose. Two more elbows in quick succession and it was a flattened, bloody mess.

He sucked in a deep, rasping breath and let out a cry of rage. With a sudden burst of strength, he rolled her off of him. Angel scrambled away before he could pin her down. The man was up on his knees but instead of coming after her, he pulled an automatic pistol from his coat pocket.

Before he could so much as take aim, Angel's roundhouse kick struck him in the temple and he went limp. His eyes glazed and, like a falling tree, he slowly fell forward. Just for meanness, she added a front kick to his face as he went down. She caught him at an awkward angle, and pain shot through her ankle, but she could not stifle her feral grin. "That's what you get," she whispered.

She hesitated for a moment, wondering where the pistol had fallen and if she should search for it.

"Ulrich?" An unfamiliar voice called from down the street. A shadow appeared in the whirling snow. Resolving into the form of Ulrich's companion– the odd one who hadn't been wearing a jacket.

Still pumped from her beat down of Ulrich, Angel entertained a fleeting thought of taking the fight to this guy as well before common sense overrode adrenaline. Reminding herself that Bones was the dumb one in the family, she turned on her heel and ran.

# CHAPTER 8

Jade was already awake when Maddock rolled out of bed. The previous evening's events, followed by the news that Angel had been attacked outside the hotel had kept the wheels of his mind turning until well into the night. When they discovered the missing skulls, they knew why the men had come.

He and Bones had taken turns staying awake, though neither of them expected the men to return. They had the skulls and didn't know about the existence of the three hares disc.

He sat up, closed his eyes, and inhaled the welcome aroma of coffee. Exactly what he needed to start this cold morning.

"It's about time. I've been on the web for hours." Jade did not look up from the tiny screen of her phone which she was using to search the internet. "I've already solved the mystery while you were dreaming about... sand, or whatever it is you dream of."

"Seriously?" He sat up straight, feeling wide awake.

"No." She turned and gave him a coy smile. "But since you're awake, how about pouring me a cup of coffee."

He gave her a playful swat on the hip and rolled out of bed, sparing a moment to work out the kinks from sleeping on a mattress that was much too soft for his liking. He poured two cups of coffee: black for him, two sugars, no cream for her. He sat her cup on the nightstand on her side of the bed, opened the curtains to let in the glow of the snow-frosted city, and settled into a nearby chair.

"I do have an idea, though." Jade took a sip of coffee and regarded him over her cup. When he didn't bite, she made a mocking pout that melted into a smile. "Fine. Don't let me have any fun."

"Tell me, my wise and beautiful queen..."

"No!" She held up her hand. "Too late now. Just sit there, drink your coffee, and enjoy the fruits of my labor." She picked up the hotel notepad she'd use for her note-taking. "Aside from the message on the disc, our clues are the three hares, the wise men, and the wise and foolish virgins. Agreed?"

"I suppose you could add Bacchus to that list."

"Might as well." She made a note. "I tried combining phrases from the message with some of these clues, along with Germany and cathedrals or churches, and using them as search terms. I've come up with one place I feel good about."

"Let's hear it."

"Saint Mary's Cathedral in Hildesheim." She fixed him with an expectant look.

"Never heard of it."

"It's famous for the Bernward Doors– huge bronze doors that depict scenes from the Bible." She checked her notes. "Each door has eight panels, and one of them shows the adoration of the Magi."

"Sounds iffy." Maddock held his coffee close to his nose, savoring the aroma. "There must be tons of representations of the Wise Men all around Germany, and that's assuming the skulls are still in the country. Who knows?"

"You're such a cynic, Maddock." Jade sighed and handed him her phone. "Take a look at this. It's a picture of the Three Kings panel."

The image was impressive. The Magi were sculpted as was the Blessed Mother holding the baby Jesus, and gave the etching a three-dimensional quality. But it wasn't the scene itself that drew Maddock's eye; it was the door knocker in the shape of a lion's head that dominated the lower middle of the panel.

"You see?" Jade grinned. "I thought the mention of the word 'lion' might be figurative, you know, Jesus was the Lion of Judah. But if it's a literal clue, this is a good fit. You've got the Magi, the lion, and the cathedral. The place is filled with works of art. There's even a shrine that includes a depiction of the wise and foolish virgins. I'll wager that somewhere in there is a depiction of the three hares. What do you think?"

"It's a stretch, but I suppose it's worth a try."

"Look, I know it's not a sure thing but, the way I see it, we're on vacation and it's a place I wouldn't mind visiting anyway. What do we have to lose except a few hours in the car?"

"That works for me," Maddock said. "But I'm guessing you've forgotten what a road trip with Bones is like."

**Maddock didn't know** if it was holiday spirit or the presence of his sister, but Bones was much less annoying than usual on their drive to Hildesheim. Instead of playing his favorite car game– thinking of an obscenity that started with the first letter of every road sign they passed– he contented himself with singing Christmas songs, though his habit of changing the lyrics to make the songs off-color finally drove Angel crazy and she put a stop to it. By the time they arrived at the cathedral, even Bones was focused on the task at hand.

"We'll start by checking out the door and take it from there," Jade said. "Keep an eye out for anything with the three hares or the wise virgins."

"What about the shrine you mentioned?" Angel asked.

"We'll take a look at that too. Anything that looks promising. Just don't draw attention to yourself." Jade directed the latter comment at Bones.

"You know me. I always rise to the occasion." Bones grinned.

Maddock gazed up at the cathedral. In no way was it as magnificent as Kölner Dom. It was smaller and less elegant, and the massive repairs to the damage wrought by Allied bombers in World War II had deprived it of the aura of age that imbued so many structures of its kind. It did, however, have its own charm. The symmetry of the structure gave it an orderly feel that was pleasing to the eye, and the sand-colored stone put him in mind of home.

It was only a short walk to the cathedral's western portal and the Bernward doors. Though impressive in photographs, the sheer size of the doors, which stood at nearly sixteen feet tall, gave him pause. The artistry of these thousand-year-old castings was breathtaking. Assuming the role of tourist, Bones took out a camera and started snapping pictures of Angel. She positioned herself to screen Maddock and Jade, who, in turn, moved in for a closer look at the Three Kings.

The panel was much larger than Maddock had imagined. He had figured the doors to be closer to an ordinary size, and thus scaled down the image in his mind.

"I don't see any hares here," Maddock said.

"The clue mentions the lion. Give it a twist." Jade whispered.

"Seriously?"

"These doors are probably thick enough to hide something inside. Maybe the knocker comes off or releases a panel." She looked around, clearly nervous. "Hurry while we're alone."

Maddock took hold of the handle, feeling the cold bronze through his thin glove, and twisted.

Nothing.

He tried the other direction with no more success. He tried pushing and turning, pulling and turning, and anything else he could think of, but no dice.

"It's just a solid piece," he finally said, rocking back on his heels.

"You didn't expect it to be easy, did you?" Bones pocketed his camera and joined them at the door. "Pretty cool, though. This alone was worth the drive, but let's check out the inside."

They were disappointed to learn the cathedral was closed for renovations, though Bones declared it "no freaking problem" to slip inside after hours, should they deem it necessary, eliciting a roll of the eyes and a vow not to post his bail from Angel.

A break-in proved unnecessary. Angel located a foreman who spoke English and apparently liked flirtatious women with dark skin and big brown eyes, because, five minutes later, they were inside.

Like the exterior, the interior had a feeling of newness about it, though tempered by the classic works of art all around. The construction foreman was eager to give them an impromptu tour, showing them the high points, including the "Christ Column," a millennium-old, fifteen-foot tall cast bronze pillar that depicted scenes from the life of Jesus, and a bronze baptismal font that rivaled the pillar in its artistry.

By the time they reached the Epiphany Shrine at the east end of the cathedral, Maddock was ready to give up. They had found no representations of the three hares, the Magi, or the Wise Virgins. The shrine was their last hope. The golden shrine was reminiscent of the shrine at Kölner Dom. Among the many images on its face was one of the Wise and Foolish Virgins. And, like the Shrine of the Magi, it was sealed in a thick glass case.

"It holds the relics of the patron saints," the foreman explained. "It is very old."

Maddock and Bones exchanged glances. If they wanted to see what was inside, they would have to blast it open like the men had done back in Cologne. The idea did not sit well with Maddock. Also, something told him this was not what they were looking for. The door to the temple had been guarded by only three wise virgins while this shrine depicted all the characters of the parable, both wise and foolish. It didn't look right. He thought back to their sole clue.

*"As the lion roars for the king..."*

He had taken "the king" to simply mean Jesus, the "King of Kings." But if the allusion to the lion had been literal, why not the king as well? He turned to their guide, who was having trouble keeping his eyes off of Angel. She was playing along, though Maddock knew her well enough to see she was growing bored with the charade.

"Are there any relics or treasures from any kings here?"

The foreman cocked his head, thinking. They all fell silent, and only the distant sounds of workmen going about their business interrupted the quiet. Finally, he nodded.

"In the museum is the Kopfreliquiar of Saint Oswald. He was King of Northumbria."

"A cop what?" Bones asked.

"Kopfreliquiar." The man cupped his chin, struggling for a translation. "This," he indicated the shrine, "holds all the bones. A kopfreliquiar," he held his hands in front of him about eight inches apart, "holds only the head."

Jade beamed at Maddock. A reliquary that held the skull of a king? That was more like it. They thanked the man, who had managed to wrangle a phone number from Angel, and left the cathedral.

"Real or fake?" Bones asked his sister as they headed back out into the cold.

"Sort of fake." Angel grimaced. "I gave him Crazy Charlie's number."

"That's cold, sis. Dude was nice enough to let us in and show us around."

"Nice? You didn't notice his wedding ring?"

Maddock and Bones looked surprised while Jade and Angel exchanged a "that's a man for you" look.

"You two can find gold at the bottom of the ocean but you can't find it on the hand of someone standing a foot from you." Jade shook her head.

"Hey, just because I haven't settled down doesn't mean I've started checking to see which dudes are single," Bones protested. "Besides, we need to find Ichabod Crane." They had arrived at the museum, and he opened the door and ushered them in with a mocking bow.

"Ichabod Crane?" Jade frowned. "What are you talking about?"

"The Headless Horseman. Am I the only educated one here?"

"Ichabod Crane was the..." Jade threw up her hands and stalked inside. Bones winked at Angel, who gave him a rueful look.

"You're such a jerk," she said, "but at least you're pestering someone else for a change."

They paid the modest entry fee and found themselves alone in the museum, save for a lone employee who reminded them that the museum would close in twenty minutes. They made a show of examining various displays, but quickly found themselves at the glass case that held Saint Oswald's head reliquary. The golden artifact was an odd-looking piece- an octagonal base with a domed cover, topped by a sculpture of Oswald's crowned head. Writing ringed the bottom, with etchings in the panels. They circled the case, scrutinizing the piece.

Jade squeezed Maddock's hand and he could feel her excitement.

"Look at the crown," she whispered. "Do you see it?"

Etched in white stone on the front of the crown was the sign of the three hares!

"Okay." Maddock kept his voice level. "So how do we get to it?"

"Leave it to me," Bones said. "You three spread out and don't act so interested in this thing." With that, he sauntered over to the museum docent and struck up a conversation. In typical Bones fashion, he soon had her laughing. The two of them soon headed out to the lobby, Bones returning a few minutes later with a slip of paper in his hand.

"You got a number too," Angel said. "What's your plan, charm her and talk her into bringing you back here later?"

"Nope." Bones reached into his pocket, pulled out a

key ring, and tossed it to Maddock. "Museum's about to close," he whispered. "Call us when you're out."

"You'd better take my backpack," Jade added, slipping it off her shoulder and handing it to him, "just in case you find something."

Maddock had to laugh at his friend's resourcefulness. This just might work.

Careful not to be spotted, he slipped around the corner in the direction of the men's room. The door was propped open and a sign with the international symbol for "don't slip on this wet floor and fall on your butt" guarded the entrance. Good! He could hide inside without being found by the cleaning crew. He hurried inside, found an uncomfortable seat atop a toilet and waited for the lights to go out.

Forty long, boring minutes later, he pulled up the hood of his jacket to shield his face–he hadn't seen any security cameras, but better safe than sorry–and moved out into the darkened museum. It had been at least ten minutes since he'd heard a sound. Though he knew only a handful of German words, he was fairly certain he'd heard Bones' new friend complaining about her missing keys. He supposed she'd hitched a ride with a friend because he heard not a sound as he moved through the dark hallway.

It took several failed tries before his clumsy gloved hands found the key that opened the protective case around the Oswald Reliquary. Heart pounding, he reached inside, took hold of the cover, and lifted the lid.

It was heavy, but it slid free easily. He gingerly set the lid aside and peered down into the reliquary. The dim glow of the security lights was more than enough to show him what was inside.

The reliquary contained two skulls.

One was unremarkable, but the other was topped with a bronze crown. Unable to breathe, he lifted it out of the case and held it up so he could take a look at the head of one of the legendary Magi of the Christmas story.

The crown was fused to the skull so perfectly that it looked to be one with the bone. Aware that he should get out while the getting was good, he opened Jade's backpack and made to put the skull inside when a faint glimmer of light caught his eye.

An opaque white gem was fixed in the front of the crown and, though it defied logic, a band of light seemed to glow from within the stone itself. He frowned, turning the skull in his hands. The light flickered but did not go away. He was intrigued, but instinct told him he was fortunate to have gotten this far without being caught. He slipped the skull into the backpack, replaced the reliquary lid, and locked the case. At the front door, the flashing lights of the security system gave him pause, but there was nothing for it but to hurry. He chose what he thought was the front door key, let himself out, locked the door behind him, and tossed the keys beneath a shrub a few feet away. Maybe the owner would find them in the morning.

By the time he reached the street, the tightness in his chest had eased and his heart had stopped racing. Even if he had set off an alarm, what would the police find? The museum locked up tight and everything in order. Even if they found the keys and concluded someone had been inside, nothing was missing as far as they knew. If a security camera showed a shadowy figure messing with the reliquary display, St. Oswald's head was still in its resting place. He wondered if this was what a thief felt like when he committed the perfect crime.

He told himself it wasn't really a crime. The skull belonged to the cathedral at Cologne, and he would see to it that it was returned. But not until they solved the mystery.

# CHAPTER 9

**The knock came** again, louder and more insistent. Andre sighed and closed his eyes, inhaling a deep, calming breath. This was his time for prayer and contemplation and the church was closed. Whoever was at the door would have to come back in the morning.

He counted to ten in his head, waiting to see if the knock would come again, but it did not. Satisfied that he would not be interrupted he returned to his prayer.

The crash shattered the momentary silence and seemed to rattle Andre's very bones. He sprang to his feet and hurried from his study.

The front door stood open and a veritable bear of a man stood in the doorway. Silhouetted against the moon, he was scarcely more than a shadow blotting out the light, but as he closed the door behind him, the sight of him changed from frightening to horrifying.

Though it was evening, he wore wraparound sunglasses that did not conceal his badly scarred face. He looked like a man who almost lost a battle with leeches. What had done this to him? Some sort of plague?

The man must have seen the horror in Andre's eyes because his pockmarked face split into something between a sneer and a grin.

"This is the church of Saint Victor." The words, spoken in heavily accented French, formed a statement, not a question. His voice was a cold, low rumble from deep within his chest and sounded to Andre like boulders crashing down a hill.

"It is." Andre swallowed hard. "What can I do for you?" He supposed it was possible the man had no ill intentions, and was merely here to see the church. Andre was wrong to judge him by his appearance. He was a child of God, the same as any other. And yes, it was rude of the man to intrude, but entering a church during prayer time was far from the most grievous of sins.

"Take me to the head of Lazarus."

"You can see all of him right here." Andre nodded to the statue of Lazarus of Bethany. The venerated saint stood with his face turned toward heaven. In his left hand, he held a crosier. "You might be interested to know that, beneath this statue, are two stones from the saint's sepulchre in Bethany."

"Don't mess with me. I don't want a statue. I want the real thing."

Andre frowned. "I do not understand."

"The skull!" The man seemed to blot out the light as he came closer. "I want to see the skull of Saint Lazarus."

"The bones of Lazarus are not here." Andre felt the blood drain from his face and his stomach grow cold. "The saint died in Cyprus and his remains were later taken to Constantinople. Perhaps if you look..." The man snatched Andre by the neck, squelching his words in a vise grip.

"We know the truth. The grotto, the three hares, all of it." He pulled Andre near enough that the priest could feel his hot breath. Up close, the scarred face was even more disconcerting. He steeled his nerves, reminding himself that he was a man of God and the Spirit would protect him.

"It is a common misunderstanding," Andre gasped. "Many confuse Lazarus of Bethany with the bishop of Aix, Lazarus."

"You aren't fooling me, and if you waste one more minute of my time, you will die a slow and painful death. I want to see the head of Lazarus. Now!" He gave Andre a shove, sending him hard onto his backside. He opened his jacket to reveal the handle of a weapon. Andre knew nothing about firearms, but the sight of it was all he needed to confirm the danger he was in.

Andre had always considered his own mortality with a serenity grounded in his assurance of salvation. Of course, he had always imagined meeting his maker from his sick bed at an advanced age. The life of a priest was a secure one, at least physically. Now, for the first time in his life, he felt death staring him in the face. This man oozed evil.

"I will take you there." Andre slowly crawled to his feet. "It is not far." His heart pounding and his bowels threatening to empty, he led the man to a door on the south side of the nave. It opened onto a staircase descending down into the ancient subterranean church beneath Saint Victor. This church, untouched after nearly two thousand years, had been built by Cassianite monks in the third century. Behind him, the man switched on a flashlight and Andre began his descent. The cold air chilled him to the bone, as did the feeling of great age and power. While many people found the fortress-like exterior of Saint Lazarus dark and intimidating, it was down underground where the true darkness lay.

Andre did not care that this place had once been a church. Something was wrong down here. Perhaps it was that this place had the feel of a dungeon; or maybe the odd carvings, many of which should not be in a place dedicated to Christ. No matter how many times Andre came down here, he always felt vulnerable and unwelcome.

He passed beneath the high ceiling supported by a few round pillars, the silence broken only by the footfalls of the man behind him. Each step sounded to him like the ring of a hammer nailing the lid on his coffin. He forced himself to keep moving, and soon came to the entrance to the ancient grotto that had been the original first-century church of Saint Lazarus. A tangle of carved vines wound its way around the entrance, adding to the forbidding nature of this dark recess.

"It is in here." Andre stepped back and motioned for the man to enter.

"You first." The man's voice made it clear he would accept nothing less than total obedience.

Andre stepped inside with only the greatest reluctance. It was as if invisible hands held him back. His fear of the crypt, however, was nothing compared to his fear of the man behind him.

"Which one is Lazarus?" The man swept his beam across the two stone sarcophagi. Between them lay a stone rectangle where a third sarcophagus had once rested.

"Neither." Andre hurried on. "These were too large to move. Lazarus is here." He hurried to the back wall, cursing himself for cowardice. Keeping the secret had been a simple thing when it was only a matter of misleading researchers, but an armed man was more than he had ever bargained for. His fingers searched the rough, shadowed surface until it found what he was searching for- the odd carving of three joined hares. Some said it was a symbol of the Trinity, but Andre knew it was an evil pagan symbol. Grimacing, he pressed his hand to the hateful symbol and pushed. The stone slowly gave way. When he heard it click, he turned it to the right once, twice, three times. It locked into place and, behind him, Andre heard a grinding sound. He turned to see the foundation stone slide back, revealing a dark hole the size and shape of a grave.

The man shone his light down into the darkness where the beam fell on a small stone box inscribed with the same three hares symbol.

"Open it."

Andre did not hesitate but clambered inside, turning his ankle in the process. Trying to ignore the burning pain, he knelt down by the ossuary. He had never actually laid eyes on it before. Taking a deep breath, he took hold of the lid and heaved.

It was a struggle. He was not a strong man and the lid was heavy, but fear had his adrenaline pumping and he was able to wrestle it free and slide it to the side. Despite his terror, he could not help but feel a thrill at knowing what was inside. The air in the ossuary smelled of dust and age. Andre leaned closer to see what lay inside.

The shaft of light shone on a perfectly preserved

skull. He found he could not breathe, but it was not due to fear– that had been forgotten. He was gazing upon the remains of Lazarus himself, whom God incarnate had raised from the dead.

"Take it out and hand it to me." Despite having found what he sought, the man sounded angry.

Andre reached in and gently cupped the skull in his trembling hands. Though the air down here was cool, a solitary bead of sweat rolled off his forehead, making a crater in the dust at the bottom of the ossuary. Slowly, carefully, he raised the skull to eye level and took one long look at it before handing it over to his captor.

The man turned the skull in one hand, scowling. He shone his light back down into the ossuary.

"There's nothing else?"

"No." The fear was back. "We have only had the skull for many centuries."

The man moved the skull to the crook of his left arm, took the flashlight in his left hand, and drew his gun with his right. He leveled the weapon at Andre's head.

"What was the secret?" The bearlike voice was now a scratchy whisper. "How did he bring Lazarus back from the dead?"

Andre gaped. Did the man not know the story?

"By the power of God. He spoke the word and Lazarus rose from the dead."

A sound like a thousand thunderclaps erupted in the crypt and fire lanced through Andre's leg. He slumped to the ground clutching his wounded thigh. He had never dreamed such pain was possible.

"Last chance to live," the man snarled. "What is the secret? How was he brought back?"

"I only know what the scriptures tell us." Andre's voice was a whimper. "I do not know any secret."

"Are you sure?"

Andre nodded. "I know nothing. Please, let me go."

The flashlight winked out, leaving them in absolute darkness. Pulse pounding in his ears, Andre strained to listen for any sounds, hoping to hear receding footsteps that would mean his terror and suffering were at an end. Silently he prayed, eyes squeezed shut. He heard the soft tread of footsteps and then...

No!

The loud scraping of stone on stone filled the room. He tried to get to his feet, but his wounded leg betrayed him and he fell down hard. Summoning all his remaining strength, he hurled everything he had into the effort, and sprang to his feet.

Pain exploded in his head as he cracked the top of his head on hard stone, and he crumpled to the ground. Head swimming and ears ringing, he tried to push himself up, but his strength was gone. Only a moan of pain and desperation escaped his lips as the stone cover slid back into place, entombing him where the saint had once lain.

# CHAPTER 10

"Let me take another look at the skull." Maddock reached into the back seat and accepted the skull from Angel. He sat it in his lap, its face grinning up at him. The Magi, the Wise Men who visited the baby Jesus in Bethlehem. Could it be true? He had to laugh. How many times in the past few years had he wondered that very thing? Either the world was jam-packed with mysteries and secrets or he and Bones were very lucky– or unlucky, depending on how you looked at things.

"I don't know what to make of it." Jade leaned over his seat to get a better look. A moment later, Angel's face joined hers.

"Hey chicks, we're driving on a snowy highway. Put your seat belts back on!" Bones shook his head. "And they say I'm reckless."

Angel laid a hand on his shoulder. "We just trust your driving ability, that's all."

Bones rolled his eyes but dropped the issue.

"Does that light ever go out?" Angel pointed to the stone set in the front of the crown.

"I think it's just reflecting light from the dashboard," Jade said.

"I'm not so sure." Maddock remembered his first impression when he removed the skull from its reliquary. The light seemed to come from within the stone. "I could see a glimmer of light in it from the very start."

"A stone that generates its own light? Maddock, that's impossible."

Maddock and Bones exchanged a quick glance. They remembered a temple underneath the earth lined with stones that could absorb and amplify light. "I once saw something along those lines, though not quite the same." He told them about what he and Bones had found in the

Holy Land a few years earlier. "I have an idea. Bones, can you pull the car over and kill the lights?"

A few minutes later they sat on a dark, deserted stretch of highway. They all huddled around the skull, blocking any ambient light, and peering intently at the opaque gem.

"I see it!" Jade gripped Maddock's arm. "There's a faint sliver of light there."

"It's almost shaped like a triangle," Angel mused. "See how it's narrower at one end?"

"But is it generating its own light, or is it like the stones we saw before, and just using the light it absorbs?" Bones asked.

"This isn't like those stones." Maddock shook his head. "Those took a little bit of light and multiplied it. This is just a sliver that seems to come from within the stone itself. Weird."

Just then, Jade's cell phone rang, interrupting their quiet contemplation. She glanced at the screen and smiled.

"It's Otto."

The conversation was brief, and Otto must have done most of the talking because Jade's contribution consisted primarily of "okay" and "uh-huh." When she hung up, she was smiling ear-to-ear.

"What was that all about?" Maddock asked.

"Otto thinks he's solved another of the clues. Paderborn Cathedral has a well-known three hares window. That by itself wouldn't help us out much, but it also houses the remains of Saint Liborius." She paused for effect.

"This conversation is already feeling laborious." Maddock grinned. "Cut the suspense."

"He was a bishop of the late fourth century during a time paganism was strong in this part of the world. Legend has it, when the relics of *Liborius*," she emphasized the correct pronunciation, "were brought to Paderborn, a peacock led the procession."

"The peacock be your guide." Maddock quoted the

passage from the clue. "Well, I guess we're headed for Paderborn."

**The west tower** of the Paderborn Cathedral rose above the ornate Romanesque-Gothic church like a sentry on the lookout for intruders. At least, that was how Maddock felt as he gazed up at the structure that stood three hundred feet. It was, to him, the cathedral's most impressive feature, though he was also blown away by the many large arched windows that contained within them smaller, narrower arched windows topped by round, highly decorative portals. No matter how many cathedrals he visited, the architecture and craftsmanship never ceased to amaze him.

"So, what exactly are we looking for?" Bones asked.

"There are two key connections to the clue," Jade said. "The three hares, and the peacock. Paderborn Cathedral has a famous three hares window. Let's start there."

They circled the cathedral examining all the windows for the three hares sign. They drew a few odd glances but probably due more to Bones' presence than their interest in the stained glass. They had searched for a half-hour before Jade decided to ask for help. They were directed to an inner courtyard where they found the three hares window and more.

"This has got to be it!" Jade exclaimed as soon as they were alone. It was not as impressive as Maddock had expected. The three stone hares in a circle were set atop a stained glass window and in front of it stood...

"A peacock!" Angel brushed the snow off of the dark stone fountain surmounted by an ornately carved peacock. "This must be what the clue was talking about."

"Could be," Maddock said. "Bones, you keep an eye out in case somebody comes this way. The rest of us will see what we can find."

They scoured the courtyard, paying particular attention to the area around the stained glass window and around the peacock fountain. The window offered no promising leads, so they focused on the peacock, but no amount of poking, prodding, pushing, or twisting uncovered any hidden compartment or passageway, nor did they find any telltale three hares images like those they had found in Cologne and Hildesheim.

They expanded their search, checking the walls around the courtyard and scraping away snow and ice from the ground in any likely spot. Maddock scrubbed rough blocks until his gloves began to tear, but with no success.

"I don't think this is the right place." He looked at Jade, who nodded. "What else did you find out about this place when you researched it last night? You know, hares and peacocks and stuff."

"If by 'stuff' you mean the Magi or the Wise Virgins, I didn't find anything. Nothing else about the three hares either." She screwed up her face in concentration. The expression made other people look constipated but, on her, it was cute. "There is supposed to be a lot of peacock imagery inside the cathedral."

"The clue talks about the peacock being the guide. A peacock supposedly guided the relics. Considering where we found the first skull, I'll bet that's the connection." He'd had a feeling about the relics, but they had wanted to eliminate the obvious first, and thus had checked the area around the three hares window.

Jade nodded. "It's the next best possibility, if not the best. The relics are down in the crypt. Let's check it out."

The Paderborner Dom featured three parallel aisles, all reaching the height of the roof. The stained glass windows that ran the length of the side walls cast the interior in a warm glow. Christmas trees hung with white lights added to the cheer. Jade took Maddock's hand and leaned her head on his shoulder.

"It's nice, isn't it?"

He nodded. It was all too easy to get caught up in the mystery and not enjoy the moment. Bones and Angel seemed to feel the same way. Each was smiling and taking in the beauty that surrounded them. The cathedral, not one of Germany's most famous or popular, was almost empty today, with only a handful of people wandering about.

Angel's face suddenly froze. She ducked behind a column and beckoned to the others.

"The guys who attacked me are here. The dark-haired one is Ulrich; I didn't get the other guy's name."

Maddock didn't need her to point out the two men who stood at the crossing looking around. If he had not remembered what they looked like, the black-haired man's battered face stuck out like a sore thumb.

"What are they doing here?" Bones scowled at the men. "Do you think Otto told them?"

"No way," Jade said. "He told them about the three hares, remember? They're probably checking out any cathedral with a three hares symbol."

"And considering what they did at Kölner Dom, they're probably going for the shrine. You two," Maddock said to Jade and Angel, "get back to the car and wait for us."

"Not a chance." Angel shook her head. "You ain't the boss of me."

"Same here, Maddock," Jade added. "Cut the chivalrous crap. You know I hate it."

"Fine." Maddock eyed the men who were slowly moving toward the east end of the cathedral. "You two keep out of sight and look for peacocks and anything else that might be promising, just in case we're wrong about the shrine. Let's go Bones." His friend nodded and they made their way through the nave, eyes on their quarry. The men were moving faster now, presumably headed for the crypt.

The columns that supported the roof were huge and it was easy to remain out of sight as they stalked the two men. Their quarry disappeared down a flight of stairs where a sign read DIE KRYPTA. A few lines in German followed. He recognized the name *Liborius* and the words *"please do not."* At the bottom, *"Silence Please"* was written in English.

Not a problem, he thought.

At the bottom of the stairs, Maddock peered around the corner, seeking the two men. What he saw took him by surprise. The crypt, Jade had told them, was one of the largest in Germany– more than one hundred feet long, but he still was not prepared for the sight. The ornate columns, arched ceiling, and tiled floor made the place look like a church beneath a church. Indeed, the space to his left appeared to be a small worship area complete with pews, a confessional, and an altar. To their right, a gated archway opened into a dark, gloomy place where the tomb of Saint Liborius lay and, directly across from them, a second set of stairs led back up into the cathedral.

The chamber in which the saint's remains were held had a semicircular ceiling that reminded Maddock of a Quonset hut. The faint light danced off the ornate walls, casting the space in a bluish glow. A representation of the saint was carved on the lid of the stone tomb. Beyond the tomb, beneath a stylized representation of peacock feathers, an arched doorway led into a second, smaller chamber, where a low plexiglass wall guarded a golden shrine.

Maddock was surprised at the lack of security afforded to Liborius's remains compared to that of the Shrine of the Magi, but he supposed the Three Kings were just a bit more famous. As that thought passed through his mind, the two men appeared from either side of the doorway in the back chamber. One of them took a quick look around to see if they were alone, then nodded to his companion. They vaulted the plexiglass wall and approached the golden shrine.

Bones took a step toward the tomb, but Maddock held him back.

"We have to assume we're outgunned. Take up positions outside the door to the first chamber and we'll jump them on the way out."

Bones grinned. He loved a good brawl.

They moved like shadows, eyes never leaving the

men in the burial chamber, who were now lifting the lid off the shrine.

"Gottverdammt!" The dark-haired man with the bruised face swore. "Es ist hier nicht!"

Maddock's German vocabulary was sufficient to get the gist of the words– *It is not here.* He looked at Bones who arched an eyebrow and nodded. He'd understood too.

Inside, the men replaced the lid and clambered back over the barrier. "Das grab?" the blond man asked. His partner nodded and they moved to the tomb of Liborius. Maddock moved back from the doorway so he would not be spotted and listened until grunting and scraping told him the men were hard at work trying to remove the lid.

A sudden crash shattered the silence.

"Dummkopf!"

Maddock grinned. These two were having a bad day. He stole a glance into the chamber and saw that the blond-haired guy, apparently worried that someone had heard the noise, had drawn his gun.

His partner inspected the tomb for a long time, moving things around and muttering under his breath. Finally, he let out a long sigh. "Nichts."

The blond man sagged visibly, pocketed his weapon, and indicated that they should replace the lid. They set to the task with angry expressions on their faces.

"Let's go." Maddock mouthed the words to Bones, who nodded. No sense in picking a fight if the bad guys were on their way out. Before they could head up the stairs, though, he heard the lid slam into place and footsteps echoed in the crypt. He ducked into a nearby alcove, hoping Bones had hidden too, rather than let his usual fight response take over. He breathed a quick sigh of relief as the men passed his hiding place without so much as a sideways glance, and mounted the stairs up into the cathedral. His relief was short-lived, however, for it suddenly occurred to him that Jade and Angel were alone and unarmed in the cathedral. He had told them to keep out of sight, but this was Jade and Angel. With a grimace, he slipped from his hiding place and followed.

# CHAPTER 11

"**I'm beginning to** think this is a dead end." Angel looked down at the English language brochure, searching for any clue they might have missed.

"It can't be." Jade stood with her hands on her hips, scowling at the big stained glass window in the cathedral's east wall as if it was somehow at fault. "The connection is too perfect. The hares, the peacock, this has to be it."

"We've looked at every peacock in this place and found nothing." Angel wasn't sure why Jade got under her skin so badly. She was actually pretty cool–quick-witted and not too girly. She supposed it was worry over Bones and Maddock that had her on edge. "I think we should check on those two."

"They're fine." Worry painted Jade's face, but she shook her head. "Whatever you might think of your brother, neither of them are dumb, and they've been through plenty of dangerous situations before. They won't let themselves get into serious trouble."

"You're sure about that?"

"I have to be. If the bad guys didn't kill us, Maddock would. He knows what he's doing. Let's just keep looking." Jade turned about slowly. "Anywhere we haven't looked?"

"How about this Trinity Chapel? The hares are a Trinitarian symbol and there were three Magi." She shrugged.

"Sounds good," Jade agree. "Let's do it."

There was not much to the chapel. Its most prominent feature was a gilded relief of Liborius himself, set in a niche between a window and a pillar. The saint held a staff in his left hand and a book, presumably the Bible, in his right.

"What are the three things on top of the Bible?"

Angel cocked her head to the left. "Rocks?"

"Rocks, stones. They symbolize healing. He's the patron saint against gallstones."

Angel guffawed. "No, seriously."

"I'm not kidding. Think about how bad it must have been to have gallstones back in the Middle Ages."

Angel took a closer look at the odd sight. A saint of gallstones! It sounded like some ridiculous crap Bones would make up. She ran her fingers across the stones and, as they passed over the center stone, she felt something. She frowned and leaned in close. There was a faint shape there! Heart pounding, she beckoned for Jade.

"Check this out!"

"What is it?" Jade's eyes popped when she saw what Angel was pointing at. "The three hares! It's faint, but definitely there." She grinned at Angel. "Want to do the honors?"

Angel put two fingers on the stone and pressed down. It resisted at first, but when she put all her strength into it, it slid back into the wall. The Liborius relief swung forward, revealing a small alcove containing a stone box. It was small, but not too small to hold a skull– even a crowned one. More nervous than she'd ever been before one of her fights, Angel removed the box and held it out for Jade to see. The three hares were engraved in the top.

"This has got to be it." Jade's low voice trembled with excitement. "You found the second skull!"

"We thank you for that." The voice startled them, and they whirled about to see the two men who, two nights before, had accosted Angel, standing with guns trained on them. "Now give us the box." The blond man grinned at her and held out a hand.

"I see your friend isn't smiling." Angel glanced at the dark-haired man's battered face. "Tell you what. I'll fight you for it. Hell, I'll fight both of you. Put away your guns and take me on like men."

"Let's kill them, Niklas," the dark-haired man said,

ignoring her. Gun trained on Jade, he moved closer to her. "I'll start with this one. I think I'll shoot her in the gut. Make sure she dies slowly and painfully."

Jade stared at him, wide-eyed, not daring to move.

"Calm yourself Ulrich," his partner said. "If they give us the box, no one need get hurt."

Angel could see the lie in Niklas' eyes. "First, you back away from my friend. Let her leave. Then I'll give you the skull."

"Angel, no!" Jade protested.

"Quiet!" Niklas snapped. "If we shoot you now, we will take the skull and still be away before anyone notifies die Polizei. I would prefer to leave here quietly, but it is not necessary." He tightened his grip on his gun.

Angel saw him swallow hard. She had a feeling the guy wasn't really a killer, but he was still dangerous.

"Fine." She kept her face blank, though her heart was pounding with fear and excitement in equal measure. "Here you go."

She heaved the stone box in his direction. After years of training with a medicine ball, the weight of the box was nothing. She didn't throw it at Niklas but tossed it over his head.

As the men turned their heads to follow the flight of the box, and Niklas moved to catch it, Bones, who had crept up behind Niklas, drove his fist into the man's face, sending him crumpling to the floor. Ulrich whirled about, pistol upraised, but Maddock stepped out from behind a pillar and cracked him across the back of the head with a candelabra.

"Nice job delaying them while we got into position." Maddock wiped the candelabra with his shirttail and dropped it the ground.

"We weren't delaying for you," Angel said. "We were just delaying. I didn't even see you until Bones popped out from between those pews and motioned for me to throw the box."

"We're SEALs." Bones retrieved the stone box and held it up for inspection. "All part of the training."

"You did a lot of in-church camouflage work in the service?" Jade kissed Maddock on the cheek, which sparked an unexpected flare of jealousy in Angel. What the hell? Maddock was like a brother to her. She supposed she'd feel protective of Bones if he ever got serious with someone.

"These guys will be coming to any minute." Maddock scooped up Ulrich's pistol and tucked it in his inside jacket pocket. "Let's get out of here."

Bones grabbed the other dropped weapon, and the four of them headed for the exit. Angel paused long enough to give Niklas and Ulrich each a kick in the groin.

"Two down," she said to herself and chuckled. Skulls or bad guys? It fit either way.

# CHAPTER 12

"There's something weird about these skulls." Maddock had been examining stones set in the matching crowns on the two skulls and the odd phenomenon of the internal lights continued. "The lights are still here and they're getting brighter."

Bones glanced over from the driver's seat. "They haven't seen the light in who knows how long. Maybe they're absorbing the light."

"Maybe, but they get brighter when they're closer together."

"Let's see," Jade said from the back seat.

Maddock held the skulls up and slowly moved them apart, then together again. Sure enough, the light dimmed as they moved away from each other and glowed brighter as they came back together. Maddock pursed his lips. "There's something else, though. You know how we noticed the light looked sort of like an arrow? Well, they both look like that and, get this, no matter how you turn them, the arrow always points in the exact same direction." He demonstrated, first with one skull, then with two held side-by-side.

"Are they like compasses?" Angel asked.

"They seem to work that way, but which way are they pointing?"

"Bethlehem." Bones' expression was serious. "Maybe the star the Wise Men followed wasn't literal."

"I swear I've heard a legend of a compass stone," Jade mused.

"The Vikings supposedly had one." Maddock had always enjoyed reading about early sailors and expeditions, and the Vikings had been among his favorites. "They called it a sunstone because it pointed the way to the sun on a cloudy day."

"But these stones aren't pointing toward the sun."

Bones took another quick glance at the skulls. "Looks like they're pointing south to me. My vote is either Bethlehem or a reverse compass pointing to the South Pole."

"Or we're reading them backward and they're just plain old compasses. That would be the simplest explanation." Jade took one of the skulls from Maddock so she and Angel could have a closer look.

"Yeah, but simplest isn't funnest," Bones griped.

"Funnest? Bones, do you even know what you sound like?" Angel sounded exasperated, but her amused smile told a different story.

"I sound like a guy who doesn't have a stick up his butt."

Maddock had to laugh. Bones and Angel were definitely the brother and sister he never had and wasn't completely sure he wanted, but they were fun.

"All right, let's put the skulls away. We're there."

The Catholic University of Eichstatt-Ingolstadt was the only Catholic university in the German-speaking world. Its history dated back to a sixteenth-century seminary, and some digging had produced the name of one of their faculty members, August Adler, as an expert on local Magi lore. They hoped he might be able to provide them with some clues that weren't easily found through an internet search.

"Call me crazy," Angel said, looking out the window, "but even with this crazy mystery, this place sort of puts me in the Christmas spirit."

Indeed, the snow-covered forests and mountains of Bavaria were some of the most beautiful Maddock had seen. It almost made him want to forsake the search and settle down in a warm pub in front of a cheery fire and let the holiday spirit wash over him. Almost.

"I know this isn't the Christmas trip you guys signed up for." Jade bit her lip.

"Nope, this is better." Bones looked as happy as he ever had. Though he loved a relaxing good time as much as the next guy, like Maddock, he was happiest when on the trail of something lost, be it a shipwreck or an artifact.

"I'm cool with it," Angel added. "I'm starting to see why you guys let yourselves get hooked up in these sorts of things. I feel so... alive."

"Facing death does that to you," Maddock said, admiring the campus, now almost empty with students on holiday. "It makes you appreciate the little things." Out of the corner of his eye he caught Jade gazing at him with a strange expression on her face. There would be plenty of time later to figure out what was on her mind. Right now, they had an appointment to keep.

August Adler was a short, stocky man with wavy white hair and a bushy salt and pepper mustache. He reminded Maddock of Mark Twain, if Twain were an aging German professor of theology. He ushered them into his office, where dark wooden shelves sagged under the weight of books stacked double.

"I understand you are all archaeologists?" He settled into his chair and placed his folded hands on his cluttered desk.

"Three of us are," Jade said, not adding that Maddock and Bones were marine archaeologists.

"Odd man out." Angel waved. "I'm just along for the ride."

"Very good." August nodded. "Tell me how I can be of help."

"We are interested in legends surrounding the Magi."

Adler frowned. His bushy eyebrows looked like two aging caterpillars performing calisthenics. "I assume you have heard about the theft of the bones from the Shrine of the Magi from Kölner Dom." A note of suspicion rang in his words.

"We did." Jade nodded gravely and the others followed suit. "That was terrible."

"What is your interest in the Magi?"

"It's really for me. I'm researching the connection between the Three Wise Men and the three hares symbol."

"Aha!" Adler relaxed visibly and leaned back in his chair. "A very interesting subject, but only to me. I assume you have read my paper on the subject."

"I just learned that the paper existed, which is how we found you. Since we were in the area, I couldn't miss the opportunity to meet you, though I would love to read your paper." Jade flashed her smile, just warm enough to melt a man's heart like butter.

"I will give you a copy before you leave." Adler took a deep breath and looked up at the ceiling, collecting his thoughts. "The connections between the hares and the Magi are speculative. The hare has long been associated with mythology and imagery of the divine. It symbolizes fertility, renewal, and new birth. The rabbit was adopted as a symbol of Easter due to its connection with a pagan fertility goddess of the same name whose festival was celebrated in the spring. The three hares are a pagan symbol, though the church adopted it, like so many other pagan symbols, as an emblem of the Trinity. Like the Magi, the origins of the symbol are unknown, but they have been found across Europe and the Far East."

"The Magi came from the east," Maddock commented.

"So it is believed." Adler nodded and went on. "Little is known about the Magi and, to be honest, scholars take little interest in them compared to other figures in the Bible. They appear only in a single gospel. Consequently, many consider them to be a fabrication inserted by the author in order to make the Nativity story better fit Old Testament prophecy. For that reason, a scholar is left to gather rumors and legends about them, nothing more."

"Could you tell us about them?" Jade asked, scooting closer to his desk. "We're interested even in the far-fetched stories."

"The more mundane legends hold that they returned to their lives in the east, or wherever they supposedly hailed from. The most unusual legend I uncovered is actually one I grew up hearing in the small village in

Upper Bavaria where I was born and raised. The legend holds that the Magi were not kings, but pagan magicians, and they left the Holy Land on a sacred task set before them by God Almighty."

"What kind of task?" Bones interjected.

"It depends on who is telling the story." Adler grinned. "Some say the three gifts to the Christ child were actually items of great power that had to be hidden from humankind. The gift of gold represented alchemy. Frankincense has been called everything from Magic dust to the dust from which mankind was created. Myrrh was an embalming oil, so it has been rumored to grant the power of resurrection. Other legends are less specific, but all agree they were hiding a great power, perhaps to preserve it until the end of days." He rolled his eyes. "This is where the legend of the Magi crosses paths with the three hares. If the legend is to be believed, the Magi hid their secrets somewhere in the Alps, and the three hares became the symbol of the cult of the Magi. Three magicians, three hares..." He shrugged.

"What about the story of the Wise Men following the star? Any legends surrounding that or is it taken at face value?" Maddock was thinking about the compass-like stones.

"The serious scholars have always tried to connect it to an astronomical event– a convergence of planets and stars. The legends have suggested that the star was actually a light the wise men carried that shone toward Bethlehem. Another story is that the star was a jewel that pointed the way."

"Like a compass stone?" Angel asked.

"Very much so." Adler nodded. "You did ask for the most far-fetched stories. Those hold that the star was taken away from Bethlehem and hidden away. One story claims that the star is hidden in a cavern deep below the Arabian Desert and can be identified by the smoke that pours up from the ground. The local version, of course, places the star in a cavern in the mountains."

"In my research, I uncovered a riddle that I believe is

connected to the Cult of the Magi." Jade looked uncertain, probably hoping he would not ask where she found the riddle. Maddock wasn't worried. Jade was good at thinking on her feet. "Can you think of any place this might be referring to? It would be a place connected with the three hares or the Magi. Probably both." She recited a passage from their clue. *"Into the depths of the well. The kings point the way to the falling ice..."*

Adler stiffened. "Are you perhaps playing a joke on me?"

"Not at all." Jade's voice was soft and reassuring. "I take it this means something to you."

Adler's eyes bored into hers and she looked him in the eye. He stared at her for the span of five heartbeats before appearing to make his mind up about something.

"Forgive me. The words were unexpected." He swiveled around and plucked a book off the shelf. Its cover was worn with age, but Maddock could read the title stamped on the cover in faded gold letters.

*Drekonhas.*

"My home," Adler explained. "Its coat of arms is a triskelion–   three connected legs. This was not always the case. Historically, the coat of arms was the three hares." It was as if a veil of sadness was suddenly drawn across his face. "The Nazis changed that when they came to power. The swastika became the new symbol until after the war."

"Why didn't they go back to the three hares?" Bones asked.

Adler took a deep breath. "My village is deep in the mountains. Even today they are a superstitious lot and undercurrents of paganism run strong among its people. The leaders viewed a return to three hares symbol as a return to the backward ways of the old world. The current symbol is more... common." He looked up at them and his face brightened. "I see a connection to your riddle for a few reasons. There is an ancient stone engraved with the three hares. It now stands beside the town hall but, prior to the rise of the Nazis, it was part of the old village well, and had been for centuries." He leaned forward and his voice fell, as if what he was about to tell them was a secret.

"As I told you earlier, Magi lore is strong in my village. The name, Drekonhas, contains parts of three words: Dreis, konig, hasen. The three king hares." He swallowed hard. "Also, there is the eisbruch."

"I'm sorry?" Jade frowned.

"Icefall," Adler explained.

"An icefall is almost like a waterfall of ice," Maddock explained. "They don't move like water, but they move faster than a glacier. They can be climbed, but they form crevasses and are filled with fractures, making them potentially deadly for climbers."

"Exactly." Adler nodded. "Drekonhas is nestled in the mountains near Sternspitze– one of the tallest peaks in Germany. Below and all around it is karst." He looked up at the ceiling and tapped his cheek with his forefinger. "How would you say it? Soft stone... no..." He shook his head. "It is filled with caves. You know limestone caves?" They all nodded. "Legend tells us that a cave beneath Sternspitze is the final resting place of the Magi's secret, and that path lies beneath the icefall."

"Has anyone tried to find it?" Maddock's heart was pounding. The idea of climbing an icefall was as exciting as it was foolish. One look at Bones told him his friend was as eager to climb as Maddock was.

"A few. All have failed. Some have lost their lives on the icefall; others returned having found nothing remarkable. Others still have sought a way in through some of the caves in the karst, but that has proved deadlier." He grimaced. "The caves go on forever, they say. They are like a warren, which is fitting, I suppose. In some places, the way grows too narrow to pass. In others, the ceiling or floor is weak and will give way under pressure. So many have failed to return that few venture there at all anymore, and those who do restrict themselves to the outermost passages." He lapsed into a brooding silence.

"I get the feeling there's more to the story," Jade said.

"Only more foolishness." Adler barked a laugh and turned to stare out the window. "It is said the caves are guarded by Krampus."

"The Christmas guy?" Jade laughed. She saw the puzzled expressions on the others' faces. "According to Alpine tradition, Krampus is a partner to Saint Nicholas. Saint Nick rewards the good children while Krampus warns or punishes the bad."

"The Anti-Santa?" Angel laughed. "What is he? A fat dude in a black suit? Deliverer of coal and fruitcake?"

"No, he's a hairy, horned man..." Jade fell silent, her face ashen.

"Are you all right?" Adler reached out and took her hand. "It must be the heat in here. Open a window, young man." He nodded at Bones and inclined his head toward the window. Maddock felt poleaxed. None of the earlier revelations had been much of a surprise, but having seen the horned skulls with his own eyes, he knew Adler's story had a kernel of truth.

"Do you believe in, like, the Yeti and stuff?" Bones asked. His awkward question an attempt to jump-start the stalled conversation.

"I do not know." Adler shrugged. "But, though I would not admit it to most people, I believe in Krampus for one very good reason."

"What is that?" Maddock's heart was hammering his ribs like a blacksmith at the forge.

"I saw him." Adler paused as if waiting for them to scoff. When they remained silent, he went on. "When I was a young man, young enough to believe in the impossible, but old enough to be a skeptic, I ventured deep into the caves below Sternspitze. I could have died, but something made me turn back." He paled and his voice grew suddenly hoarse. "Something peered around a corner and looked at me just as I am looking at you. A hairy man with horns."

"Could you have been mistaken?" Angel asked. She seemed to be searching for a reason not to believe the skulls came from real creatures. "A shadow on an oddly-shaped rock or something?"

"Does a rock have glowing eyes that reflect a flashlight beam? I know what I saw, and I have never gone back." Adler's gaze turned flinty, and his countenance grew cold. "I fear that is all I can tell you. I hope you will exercise caution if you investigate the subject any further."

They thanked him for his help, and he assured them it was no problem. He spared a minute to print out a copy of his paper on the Magi cult and then saw them out.

Maddock could not stop thinking about the mountain, the icefall, and the mysterious caves below. "Professor Adler, does Sternspitze have a meaning?"

Adler gave him a wry smile. "As a matter of fact it does. It means star spike."

**Ubel Karsch heard** footsteps on the other side of the door. He hurried across the hall, slipped inside his office, and peered out through the small window set in his door. He watched as Adler saw his visitors out, and what a group they were: two men, one of them the biggest American Indian he had ever seen, the other a blond man whose serene face stood at odds with the danger he exuded with every step. Both of them had a military bearing about them, though the big Indian tried to hide it with his ridiculous motorcycle jacket and juvenile t-shirt. The women were unusual too– one American Indian and one Asian.

It was not the strange visitors he cared about, though. It was the story Adler had told them. In the seven years they had worked together, Ubel had probed him on many occasions for legends about the Magi, and the old fool had never told him the legends surrounding his own home town.

He grimaced. How would his news be received? Would he be praised for finally ferreting out this new information, or would he be treated as a failure for having taken so long to uncover it? It made no difference. There was nothing he could do now except make the call and hope for the best.

He looked up and down the hallway, making certain no one was about. He turned on the radio and turned it toward the door. "We Three Kings" wafted from the speakers. Fitting.

Heart pounding and throat tight, he punched up the number. When someone picked up on the other end, he spoke the two words that would gain him immediate access to his Elder.

"Heilig Herrschaft."

# CHAPTER 13

**Drekonhas was the** epitome of the classic Alpine village. Nestled amongst the snow-capped mountains, the place made Maddock feel like he'd been sent back in time. The morning sun set everything aglow. Except for the occasional vehicle they passed, the scene was like something out of a picture book.

"This is a pretty cool place. I wonder where the Burgermeister Meisterburger lives." Bones turned toward Maddock. "What's the plan?"

"Make like tourists," Maddock said, pulling into a parking space near a small pub. "Bones, you hit the pub and see if you can meet up with anyone talkative, preferably an old-timer. See what you can learn about the caves and the icefall." Bones fist-pumped. "Two things," Maddock added. "Don't get too pushy with the questions, and take sips, not gulps."

"Dude, I know the drill. When it comes to pubs, this is not my first rodeo."

"Oh, and don't get distracted by any babes you might meet."

Bones rolled his eyes. "Yes, Dad."

"Angel and Jade, you check on lodging and do a little browsing in the shops. Act like normal visitors. I'll scope out the well. If it looks like a one man job and no one's around, I'll take care of it myself and we'll move on to the next phase. I think the stones in the crowns are compass stones and they're pointing the way to whatever is under the icefall." They had purchased climbing gear and warm clothing in anticipation of climbing Sternspitze. "If not, Bones and I will have to go back after dark."

"I don't like you going by yourself, Maddock," Jade said. "Let one of us go with you. It doesn't take two to see if there's 'room at the inn.'"

"No offense, but you three will stand out like crazy in a German village. I'm a blue-eyed blond. The only thing conspicuous about me is my good looks."

Jade rolled her eyes but relented. The three of them left the car and spread out. Maddock waited for them to disperse before heading for the old village well.

Jade checked her watch as she stepped outside of the cozy inn where she'd managed to secure the last available rooms. She glanced at her watch. That hadn't taken long. She'd meet up with Angel, wander the village for a little while. Maddock shouldn't need more than an hour. Then they could firm up their plans.

She ignored the shiver of worry that passed through her as she thought of Maddock out on his own. He was as solid a man she'd ever known—smart, capable, and resilient. He wouldn't get himself into anything he couldn't handle.

Snow crunched underfoot as she wandered through the town, returning the occasional wave. Adler had made Drekonhas sound like a small, secluded pocket of paganism, sort of an Alpine version of *Deliverance*, but it didn't seem to be the case. It was bigger than the "village" she had pictured in her mind, and seemed tourist-friendly. The woman at the inn had been pleasant enough, and there was a warm, friendly vibe about the town. The mystery notwithstanding, this might be a fine place to spend Christmas.

A strong hand seized her by the arm.

"Quit messing around Bones." She turned and what she saw made her jaw drop.

"Hello, Ihara. Missed me?"

Sunglasses and a scarf hid much of his face, but she knew him immediately.

"Issachar!" She froze in shock for only an instant, but that was her undoing. Before she could lash out with a punch or kick, he yanked her toward him and crushed her in a bear hug.

"Isn't this nice? Two old friends reunited."

His warm, damp breath on her ear and his sickly sweet tone turned her stomach. She squirmed, trying to break free, but he held her so tight that she could not move an inch. He held her face pressed into his coat, preventing her from crying out... or breathing.

"Thought you got rid of me out in the desert, didn't you? I'm not so easy to kill. Your friend Maddock will find that out soon enough, but first, I have a job to do and you're going to help."

Jade tried again to fight, stamping down on his foot, but he avoided it with ease. She was already feeling the lack of oxygen and her strength was waning.

"Go to sleep, little traitor. You're going to need your rest."

Maddock, Bones, Angel, somebody help me! Her thought faded as blackness overcame her.

When she came to, she was face-down in the back seat of a car. Her arms and legs were bound. Where was she? What had happened to her? Slowly, as if gluing together the pieces of a shredded picture, she remembered. And when she did, she screamed. At least, she tried to scream, but all she managed was a weak cry. The vehicle backed up fast, sending her rolling forward, and she found herself wedged between the seats, not quite down on the floorboard. They were moving forward now. She must have been out for only a short while– long enough for Issachar to put her in the car and tie her up. She took a deep breath and called out again.

"Help! Help!" This time it was good and loud.

"Keep screaming, Ihara. This might as well be a ghost town– nobody's out on the streets this morning. In about two minutes, we'll be out of town and headed for the mountains."

Jade took him up on his offer, shouting herself hoarse and kicking the door the best she could manage considering her bonds and awkward position. Finally, she gave up.

"About time. You were drowning out my Christmas

music." Issachar's wicked laugh sent chills down her spine. "Bet you're sorry you betrayed us now."

"I didn't betray you," she wheezed. "I was never part of the Dominion."

"Doesn't matter. You're going to help us now."

"The Dominion is dead." She wanted to believe that, but knew it wasn't true. Maddock had learned a few things during his trek into the Amazon– enough to know there was more to the Dominion than they'd previously believed.

"The Deseret Dominion is dead, or close to it, but there's more to us than that. Much more. How do you think I found out about this town and the icefall? I even have a pretty good idea what this does." He held up a crowned skull. "I got to the well first."

No ice could have been as frozen as Jade's insides at that moment. "Adler told you? No way." She couldn't believe the kind old man was part of the Dominion. Then again, she'd misjudged people before on that score.

Issachar barked a laugh. "Heilig Herrschaft has plenty of eyes and ears."

Jade squeezed her eyes closed. Her head was throbbing and she still felt woozy from her lapse into unconsciousness.

"What do you want with me, Issachar? If you know about Adler, you know everything I know." Issachar was vicious enough to kill her out of revenge for what he considered a betrayal of the Dominion, but instinct told her he had a scheme and she was to be a part of it. Either possibility made her want to throw up.

"Let's just say you're going to be a litmus test. I was going to use one of those Herrschaft idiots, but this will be much more satisfying." He smiled. "Santa came early this year. It's Christmas Eve and I've already gotten a present."

# CHAPTER 14

**It was gone.** Maddock looked down at the stone etched with the three hares, lying on the frozen bottom where someone had dropped it. The space it had once filled was set at eye level. It was easily large enough to have held one of the skulls of the Magi. He took one last look, then reached inside and felt around just to make certain he had not missed anything, but he knew it was futile. Someone had beaten them to it.

Cold and angry, he made the climb back out, the frozen stones slick under his fingers. He lost his grip a few times, but managed to catch himself. Come on, he chided himself. You can't escape armed bad guys only to die falling down a well. When he finally hauled himself out, he was in a foul mood. Were the skulls essential to finding the secret that lay beneath the icefall? If so, would they need all three? He supposed it did not matter now. They would have to proceed with what they had.

"Put your hands in the air." He knew that voice. He'd heard it just a few days earlier in Paderborn.

He looked up to see Ulrich and Niklas standing there, weapons drawn, grinning. Warily, he held his hands away from his body to show he was unarmed. They had taken the skull and then set a trap for him, and he'd walked right into it.

"Give us the skull." Niklas held out his hand.

"What?" Maddock was genuinely surprised. "You already have it."

"Let us have it!" Ulrich shouted. He trembled with anger. Perhaps his battered and bruised face, which was probably a handsome one under ordinary circumstances, and the memory of the two whippings he'd already suffered at the hands of Maddock's group, was the cause of his anger. Maddock looked into his dark eyes, and saw something more; there was a deeper cause for his rage.

"We must have it. Time is almost up."

"What do you want with it?"

A wiser man would not have wasted time bandying words with Maddock, but Ulrich had already proved himself reckless, and his agitated state only amplified that trait.

"We must find the Magi! They left the key to resurrection."

"Ulrich, Nein!" Niklas snapped, but the other man rambled on.

"The Fuhrer must live!"

"Wait a minute." He tried to recall what Adler had told them about the Magi legend. "You think the myrrh will bring back a guy who's been dead for more than a half-century?"

The two men exchanged furtive glances, and Maddock's heart skipped a beat.

"No way!" It couldn't possibly be true.

Ulrich clearly realized he had said too much. His face reddened, but his eyes burned with righteous anger.

"It doesn't matter anyway. I don't have it."

"Do not play with us." Niklas sounded stern, but Maddock could see in his eyes that the man knew something was amiss. "Give it to us now."

"It's gone. If you didn't take it, someone else must have." He raised his hands a little higher. "Search me if you want. Heck, look down in the well. The stone that covered its hiding place is still lying there."

The men exchanged looks. Niklas nodded, and Ulrich approached Maddock. Pistol in one hand, he gave Maddock a light pat-down with the other. Maddock breathed a sigh of relief that the man had skulls on his mind. Otherwise, Ulrich might have given him a more thorough pat-down and discovered the Heckler & Koch USP he had lost in Paderborn and Maddock had recovered. Satisfied Maddock did not have the skull, Ulrich pushed Maddock in Niklas' direction and leaned over the edge of the well to look inside.

Maddock wouldn't get a better chance than this. He

pretended to stumble forward, then lashed out with a right cross that caught Niklas on the chin. It was a quick, clean blow that sent the surprised Niklas stumbling backward. Turning around and drawing the HK-USP, Maddock clubbed the unsuspecting Ulrich across the back of the head and then leaped to the side as bullets flew.

Niklas' shots tore through the space Maddock had occupied a moment before. Two bullets ricocheted off the old well, but the third caught the slumping Ulrich in the back, and he slid to the ground, leaving a smear of blood on the weathered stone.

Maddock rolled to his feet and pumped two rounds into Niklas' gut. No hired thug could outshoot a SEAL. He would have put another in the man's head to finish the job, but he hoped to get a few questions answered first.

He kept his gun trained on Niklas, but there was no need. The man had dropped his weapon and now held his arms pressed to his ruined belly as if he could hold the life in. He looked up at Maddock, his eyes glassy with disbelief.

"Help me," he gasped.

Maddock had seen enough wounds to know there was no hope for Niklas. He had minutes left, if that. "The only thing that can help you right now is to make things right with your maker if you believe in one."

"Of course I believe." Niklas closed his eyes and let his head fall back. "I work for Him."

"Who do you work for?"

"Heilig Herrschaft." His voice was already fading.

"What is that?"

"The Holy Dominion." He groaned and shuddered. "Hurts."

Maddock felt numb. "Are you connected to the Dominion in America?"

"America." Niklas managed a weak laugh, and bloody froth oozed onto his cheek. "So young a nation and so limited in their vision. The same is true for our

Herrschaft brethren there." He coughed weakly.

"Do you have any idea who took the last skull?"

Niklas' eyes sprang open, and for a moment he seemed fully alert. "Issachar!" he hissed.

Maddock could not hide his shock. Stunned, he wobbled to his feet and took a step back. "What did you say?"

"Issachar. That is the name of the American the Herrschaft put above us. He must have betrayed us and taken the skull for himself." The sudden burst of life was already dissipating, but Maddock understood the man's final words. "Kill him." And then he was gone.

He dumped the bodies in the well and tossed in some branches and snow to hide the bodies. He figured it wouldn't take too many more snowy days before they were hidden until the thaw. Considering the well's remote location, it might be longer before they were discovered. His mind spun as he drove back to town. How could Issachar still be alive? It had to be the same guy. How many Issachars were in the Dominion? Or in the world, for that matter?

Bones and Angel were waiting outside the inn when Maddock made it back to the center of town. Before Maddock could cut the engine, Bones had yanked open the door and hopped in.

"Don't you ever answer your phone?" Bones snapped.

"Not much reception up here. What's up?"

"Jade's gone. The innkeeper saw her with some dude. Said he was big and had a messed up face."

"Issachar." Maddock spoke the word like a curse.

"What? He's dead, Maddock. You killed him."

"He's back." Maddock's voice was as cold and flat as a frozen lake.

Shock registered in Bones' face. "If that's true, he's got Jade. The lady said it looked like she fainted and he helped her to the car and drove off."

Hot rage boiled up inside Maddock. He wanted to kill Issachar with his bare hands, feel the life drain from his body.

"Did you find out the way to the icefall?"

Bones nodded.

"We're going after her. The skulls and climbing gear are in the back. Angel, you go back to the inn and call the police."

"No way, man. I'm coming with you."

"No! The police need to know what happened. The lady at the inn can tell them what happened. Show them this." He took a picture of himself and Jade from his wallet and handed it to Angel. "They'll want a picture of her, and the lady at the inn can confirm that the guy she left with isn't me. I don't know what kind of law enforcement they have up here, but maybe they can get some help to us."

"Fine, but as soon as they've heard my story, I'm coming after you." Angel slipped out of the car. "Pop the trunk so I can get my share of the climbing gear."

Maddock looked at Bones, who shook his head. Maddock hit the auto-lock button, put the car in reverse, and backed out of the space. Angel cursed and punched the driver's window, though not hard enough to break it; she was a fighter and knew enough to take care of her hands.

"You two better make it back so I can kick your asses!" she shouted as Maddock hit the gas and shot down the frozen road.

# CHAPTER 15

"I can't make it." Jade lay where she had fallen face-down, the warm, salty taste of blood in her mouth and her cheek stinging from its impact with the ice. Issachar had untied her ankles but left her hands tied behind her back. The icefall was difficult enough to traverse without the added handicap. Already they had slid back a dozen times on the glassy surface, and they never knew when the ice would give way beneath them.

"You'll make it if I have to carry you," Issachar growled.

She was Issachar's canary in the coal mine. He made her walk in front so, if the ice gave way, she would be the one to fall. Considering he outweighed her by at least one hundred pounds, she held out hope that they'd cross a place where the ice would support her but not him. Then again, if he fell, she had no doubt he'd take her with him.

"I need my hands free if I'm going to climb."

"Not a chance. Now get up."

"I'm lying face-down on the ice with my hands tied behind my back. How am I supposed to get up?" Fiery pain burst through her skull as Issachar hauled her to her feet by her hair. He pulled out a knife and she wondered if he was going to kill her right then and there, but instead, he sliced her bonds.

"Don't try anything." He spun her around and retied her hands in front of her. "That's as good as it's going to get. Now move it."

Despite her warm clothing, the icy breeze cut through her and she found herself wishing for a quiet place to curl up and go to sleep. She dismissed the thought as a wish for hypothermia. She didn't know what sinister plan Issachar had in store, but she was determined to find a way to escape before he put it into effect. To do that, she had to stay awake and alert.

The stone set in the Magi's crown glowed brighter the higher they ascended. Following the direction the small arrow of light indicated, they found themselves at the base of an overhang. The moment they moved into its shelter, light exploded in the stone, and it shone like a tiny sun, the arrow pointing directly at the rock. Grinning, Issachar took an ice axe off his back and began hacking away at the frozen ground.

Jade wondered if she could get away now while he was down on his knees, focused on his task, but quickly dismissed the idea. He had a gun, a knife, an axe, and two free hands. Maybe she should try anyway. What other chance might she have?

Just then, Issachar broke through the ice, and warm air, at least warmer than the outside air, flowed up from the dark passageway that ran at an angle down into the mountain.

"You first." He stood, grabbed her by the back of the neck, and pushed her toward the hole.

Dropping down onto her bottom, she slid into the passage and scooted forward until the way leveled out enough that she could get to her feet. Issachar followed behind. He held the skull, gazing down at the compass stone. The light in the stone pointed straight ahead. Issachar gave her a shove and she led the way.

The glow from the stone was sufficient to light their way for a good fifteen paces up ahead, allowing her to avoid several places where the floor had broken through. She glanced down at the blackness and wondered how far a person would fall should they slip through.

As he had done on their trek across the ice, Issachar kept a few feet behind her in case she fell through. She considered running away but, assuming he didn't shoot her immediately, she'd only make it forty feet or so before she'd find herself immersed in total darkness.

They picked their way through the warren of twisting tunnels that split, rejoined, and crossed one another until she was completely befuddled. Had it not been for the compass stone, they would have been lost within minutes. Each time they came to a fork, Issachar would consult the stone and tell her which way to go. They kept going, always another turn, another passageway, and always down.

It went on that way until she found herself wondering if they'd been fooled. What if there was no secret down here? What if they wandered these passageways without ever finding their way out? The thought of dying down here in the dark with no food or water was even more horrifying than her fear of Issachar.

"What do you think you're going to find down here, anyway?" The darkness had seeped inside her and she longed for the sound of a human voice, even if it was her own... or Issachar's.

"The treasures of the Magi. One in particular."

"Gold? Magic dust? Embalming oil? What does the Dominion want with any of that?"

"Idiot! It's much more than that." He paused. "The Magi were true magicians. They had power we can only dream of."

"Such as?" She actually did want to know what Issachar believed waited for them, but she also wanted to occupy his mind as much as possible. Maybe he would make a mistake.

"The power to bring someone back to life." His hushed voice rang with reverence and wonder. "How do you think Lazarus was brought back to life? Or Jesus?"

"I thought God did that."

"It was myrrh. The little bit the Magi left as a gift was enough to resurrect two men, perhaps more! Think what I can do when I find their entire store!"

"What *you* can do?" She frowned. "What about the rest of your Heilig Herrschaft friends?"

"Heilig Herrschaft has its own plan for the myrrh, and it's an idiotic one. I don't think it would work for what they want to do and, even if it did, it's a bad idea. It goes against what the Dominion stands for."

"You're nuts." Jade meant it. She'd expected this

mystery to reveal something unusual. She thought the compass stones might point toward a deposit of the stone from which they'd come or something with at least some grounding in science, but an embalming oil that restored life?

"You had better hope I'm right."

"What do I care if you're right or not?" Up ahead, she spotted a sunken place about the width of a man. Cracks ran across it like cobwebs. Could this be her chance? She needed to keep him talking. "Take your oil and bring back whoever you like. Just let me go."

Issachar laughed. "You still haven't figured it out? I thought you were smart, Ihara."

Ten more steps.

"I have to make sure the oil is going to work before I take it back to the Herrschaft."

Jade missed a step. She turned and gaped at Issachar. He'd taken off his wraparound shades when they descended into the tunnel, and his scarred face was even more ghoulish in the glow of the compass stone.

"Look who finally caught up. I was going to used one of the two Herrschaft idiots, but it will be much more satisfying to choke the life out of you." He grinned. "Look on the bright side. If it works, you'll be the first person in two thousand years to be resurrected. Maybe you can start your own religion." He gave her a shove to get her moving. "Then again, I might just kill you twice. Double your pleasure, double your fun." He threw back his head and laughed.

Jade stepped as close as she dared to the edge of the depression, and then stepped across without breaking her stride. She closed her eyes and prayed. *Please, please, please...*

Issachar's laughter cut off into a yelp of surprise as the limestone beneath his feet shattered.

Jade looked back, expecting to see a gaping hole in the floor, but instead she saw Issachar stuck up to his armpits in the hole. He was frantically trying to push himself up and out, but he was wedged in tight. He bellowed and thrashed about, but lapsed into silence when his movement caused him to slip a centimeter. He looked up at her, his eyes shining in bewilderment.

"Get me out of here."

Now it was Jade's turn to laugh. He had dropped the skull when he fell, and she scooped it up– an awkward task with her bound hands. She looked at the tunnel behind him. There was no way she could get past him, and even stuck as he was, he was strong enough to hurt her. She would have to find another way out.

"It's been fun, Issachar, but I've got go. Don't bother to write."

"You help me, Ihara!" he cried. "Help me!"

Still too unnerved to laugh, she hurried down the passageway, his cries ringing in her ears.

# CHAPTER 16

"Looks like they were definitely here." Maddock kicked at the chunks of ice that had been cleared away from the tunnel entrance. "Somebody's hacked this up. You can tell by the marks."

"Maybe it was Krampus." Bones winked. "Relax, Maddock. We're going to get her back."

"I'm not tense; I'm focused." Maddock didn't look at Bones. His friend would see the lie in his eyes. "Let's move."

The passageways beneath the Sternspitze icefall were just as Adler has described– a confusing, twisting, turning mess that was sure to baffle even the most skilled spelunker.

"It's like walking through Swiss cheese," Bones said, running his hand along the pale limestone walls.

"Well, we are in the Alps, though not in Switzerland."

They each carried a skull and followed in the direction indicated. The stones had, so far, proved to be excellent compasses.

"Keep an eye out for holes," Maddock said. "This place doesn't seem very solid."

"Dude, I'm busy trying not to bash my head on the low ceiling. I can't win."

They picked their way through the eerie silence. Bones managed to avoid bashing his head, though he frequently complained about his sore back. Maddock suspected the complaints were his friend's way of keeping Maddock's mind off of Jade. It didn't work, but he appreciated the effort.

"Cover the stones. Quick!" Bones whispered.

The world was doused in black as Maddock and Bones put their hands over the glowing compass stones. Maddock looked all around, all his senses alive.

"What was it?"

"I saw a flash of light down that side passage. It's gone now." Bones exhaled slowly. "Think we should check it out?"

Maddock frowned. He was sure Issachar had the other skull, which meant he was probably following its compass stone. He felt their best bet was to follow wherever the stones led. That was where he hoped to find Jade and the truth behind this mystery. He explained his thinking to Bones, who grimaced.

"But what if they've already gotten there and are on their way back out."

"They'd run into us, wouldn't they?" Unless they made a wrong turn. "Fine, let's check it out."

They crept into the tunnel, each cupping a hand over their compass stone to permit only a minimum amount of light to come through. They moved forward like shadows, alert for any sound or sight that would alert them that someone– or something– approached.

And then Maddock heard it. It was a clicking sound, like a deer skittering across pavement. They froze, dousing their lights. Maddock's heart pounded and he stood, nerves tingling, ready to draw his weapon and start shooting. The noise grew louder and then ceased. He caught a faint whiff of a musky, animal scent, and then the sound faded into the distance.

"What the hell was that?" Bones muttered.

"Maybe Adler really did see something." Maddock set his jaw. Whatever it was hadn't tried to mess with them. That was a good sign.

"Go a little farther?" Bones asked.

"A little." Maddock glanced down at the compass stone on his skull, which was pointing back the way they had come. "Good thing this isn't a talking GPS."

"Make a U-turn now," Bones mimicked. He looked like he was about to continue, but his features froze.

Footsteps were coming their way and moving fast. They covered their lights and drew their pistols. Up ahead, the bend in the passageway began to glow with a faint light that grew brighter as the sound of someone moving grew louder. Now Maddock could hear heavy breathing like a marathon runner at the end of a race. He tensed.

"Make sure Jade's with him," he whispered to Bones. If it was Issachar, they'd have to try to overcome him without killing him— at least until they found out what happened to Jade.

But it was not Issachar.

"Jade!" Maddock cried when she turned the corner.

Jade screamed and dropped the skull she was carrying. The bronze crown clanked when it hit the floor. She recovered her wits instantly.

"Maddock?" she breathed.

"And his better-looking amigo." Bones uncovered his compass stone as Maddock rushed forward and clutched Jade in a tight embrace.

"Are you all right?"

"Fine. Just banged up and worn out." She pressed her cheek to his chest and he stroked her hair.

"Where's Issachar?"

"He fell into a hole in the floor and got stuck. I took the skull and ran." Her breath came in gasps. "Had to try and find a new way out. I've just been doing the opposite of what the stone told me to do."

"You're headed in the right direction, but it's a long way back," Bones said.

"I'm just glad you're all right." Maddock didn't want to let her go.

"Maddock, there's a branch of the Dominion in Germany."

"I know. You can fill me in on the way out. Let's go." He took her hand and turned to lead her back up the tunnel and was surprised when she held him back.

"Are you kidding me?" She looked from Maddock to Bones and back to Maddock, a disgusted look on her face. "I travel across Germany, get kidnaped, all to solve a stupid mystery and you don't want to see it through to the end?"

"Jade..."

"Don't 'Jade' me. You two are here now. I'm safe. Let's finish this."

Maddock hesitated. Of course, he didn't want to stop now.

"You do what you want," Jade said. "Bones and I are going. Come on, Bones." She brushed past Maddock and headed down the tunnel.

"You attract the stubbornest chicks, Maddock." Bones clapped him on the shoulder. "We might as well go with her."

Shaking his head, Maddock drew his gun and followed Jade.

As they went along, Jade recounted Issachar's belief that he would find the Magi's gift of myrrh and that it could resurrect the dead. Maddock remembered what Ulrich had told him about Heilig Herrschaft's plan, and was about to fill her in when Jade came to a sudden stop. Right in front of her a deep hole barred their way.

"Good catch." Maddock put a protective hand on her arm. "Wouldn't want to step into that."

"He was here." She knelt and shone her light into the hole. "This is where Issachar was stuck. I'm sure of it."

Maddock and Bones added their light to hers. All they could see was darkness.

"Nothing we can do about it now. We'll just have to keep an eye out." Maddock stood and hoisted Jade to her feet. Now he was even more alert, he took the lead as they moved deeper into the labyrinthine tunnels.

With each step, the compass stones seemed to shine brighter, and the tunnel filled with a bluish-white glow.

"I don't think it's the compass stones doing this," Maddock said. The glow was coming from the end of the passageway. They turned the corner and stopped dead in their tracks.

Maddock looked at his friends and then at the sight that lay before them.

"I don't believe it."

# CHAPTER 17

They stood on a ledge overlooking a yawing cavern so wide they could scarcely see the other side. Floating in midair down below them was a glowing blue-white orb. Its surface pulsed and sparkled, bathing the jagged rocks of the cavern in a pale glow. The light had an odd quality to it– though Maddock sensed an intensity to it, he could look on it without so much as squinting. And though the cavern was a comfortable temperature, the thing was obviously not giving off heat.

"What's keeping it up in the air?" Bones asked.

Maddock shook his head. He had never seen anything like it. It seemed to be a self-contained ball of pure energy. "I want to know what fuels it. It can't just burn perpetually, can it?"

"Guys, look at this." Jade held up the skull she was carrying. The stone gleamed with light the exact color and quality of that which burned below. "It's the same."

"All along, these compass stones weren't pointing to a pole." Bones scrutinized his own Magi skull. "They were pointing to this place."

"Jade, what's the German word for light?" The pieces were falling together in Maddock's mind.

"Licht," she said, mesmerized by the pulsing ball of light.

"Remember what the dying priest said? *'Ewige l...'* He wasn't saying *'eternal life,'* he was saying *'eternal light.'* He meant this light."

"Whoa." Bones took a step back. "Like how we thought the stones were making their own light! If this is a source of perpetual light..." He looked at Maddock.

"A limitless supply of clean energy without the need for fuel. Unless we're way off base." He took a deep breath, trying to envision a nation harnessing such power. Even if it was not put to any sort of military use, it could give a country's economy such a boost that it could re-allocate massive resources to its military. It would be a treasure far beyond the rumored gifts of the Magi.

Jade suddenly tugged at Maddock's wrist. "Maddock, you remember the story Adler told about the star the Wise Men followed being hidden underground! Do you," she swallowed and her voice became very small, "do you think this is the Star of Bethlehem?"

"Maybe. Or at least, it's whatever is behind the story. It's obviously not an actual star." He chuckled. "Nothing like stating the obvious, huh?"

"I wonder..."

Jade did not get to complete her thought because they suddenly found themselves surrounded by men armed with spears and arrows tipped with blue stones that shone like the ball of light down below. They had crept up silently and taken up positions in a semicircle, leaving Maddock, Bones and Jade trapped between a pit with no visible bottom and a line of armed men.

Except they weren't men.

Horns protruded from their long, shaggy brown hair, and though they appeared human, if overly muscular and hairy, from forehead to waist, they were definitely animal-like from the waist down. At the waist, their body hair grew thick and glossy, and coated their thick thighs and lean calves. Their legs, which bent backward, ended in dark, cleft hooves, like a...

"A goat," Maddock whispered. "They're satyrs." His thoughts flashed to the pagan temple beneath the cathedral in Cologne. Satyrs were associated with Dionysus, or Bacchus, depending on your preferred mythology. A creature like this was the Krampus whom Adler had seen so many years ago.

One of the goat men cocked his head at the word 'satyr,' and nodded once. He pointed and Maddock realized he was indicating the pistol tucked inside his jacket pocket. Slowly, Maddock took it out and laid in on the ground; Bones did the same. The satyr gave another nod and came forward to collect them when a loud voice rang out in the cavern.

"Nobody move or the goat dies!" Issachar emerged from a nearby passageway. His left arm was wrapped around a satyr, holding it tight. In his right hand, he held a knife pressed to its throat.

They emerged into the light of the cavern and Issachar's eyes fell on the glowing ball of energy. Unlike the others, he did not seem mesmerized or even impressed. Instead, his face contorted in rage.

"Where's the myrrh?" he screamed.

The satyrs exchanged glances, their expressions so foreign to Maddock as to be unreadable.

"It's not here, Issachar. You had it all wrong."

"I wasn't wrong." There was a pleading tone to his voice. "The secret to eternal life..."

"Eternal light!" Maddock corrected. "Ewige licht, not ewige leben."

The satyrs looked at him as if the German words were familiar. Maddock could have sworn one of them looked at Issachar with a scornful grin.

"There is a miracle here, but not the one you thought you would find." Maddock took a step forward. "Let him go."

"I don't believe you. The Magi's treasures are here."

"The one treasure is here. The Star of Bethlehem, whatever it is, but you can't take it with you. Do yourself a favor, give it up and run. You might even get away." He took another step forward and the ring of satyrs parted to make room for him.

"But Lazarus... Jesus... how did they rise from the dead?"

"I don't know." Maddock shrugged. "Maybe it was a regular old miracle. Whatever it was, you won't find the answer here." He spoke the last slowly, as if to a dimwit. "Let him go."

"What do you care about a goat?" Issachar's eyes burned with hatred.

"I don't care. I care about kicking your ass."

Maddock grinned. "Again."

"That's what I'm talking about," Bones said.

Maddock's grin split into a broad smile as rage boiled in Issachar's eyes.

"Come on," he goaded, "don't you want to get me back for what happened at Zion? Be a man."

Issachar roared like an enraged lion, but before he could make a move, the satyr he was holding raised a leg and kicked him in the shin with the force of a bucking bronco. Issachar's roar turned to a shriek of pain as his shin snapped. In a flash, six satyrs were on him. They bore him up and carried him away, still screaming, into the darkness.

The satyr who had first approached Maddock turned and stared at him. They stood there, listening to Issachar's cries fade away, and waited. There was an odd, almost expectant look in the satyr's eyes, like he was waiting for something. Maddock thought for a moment, and then realized he was still holding the Magi skull.

He held it out in front of him like an offering and then laid it carefully on the ground. Bones and Jade followed suit, and they all backed to the edge of the cliff.

The satyr folded his arms, looked down at the skulls, then took a long look at each of them, and nodded. He motioned three others forward. Each drew a knife and approached the three people standing on the cliff edge.

"What do we do?" Bones whispered from the side of his mouth.

"I think we're okay," Maddock said. "If not..." He let the words hang in the air. If not, they'd have to fight the best they could.

The satyrs stopped when they reached the skulls. Each one of them used his knife to pry a compass stone from one of the crowns. One by one, they hurled the stones into the cavern.

They looked like little meteorites, shining like little balls of pure light as the pulsing light drew them in. When the job was done, they handed the skulls back to Maddock, Bones, and Jade.

The satyr whom Maddock had come to regard as the leader now approached them. One by one, he placed his hand over each person's heart and made another of his little nods. When he was done, he pointed to the way out.

"I don't think we can find our way back," Maddock said.

The satyrs might not speak English, but they seemed to understand his doubtful tone. One of them moved to the mouth of the tunnel and beckoned for them to follow.

Their glowing spear heads showing the way, one satyr led and another followed them out through the maze of dark tunnels. The path they took was more direct than the way they had come, because it seemed in no time they were standing on a snow covered ridge looking down on the twinkling lights of Drekonhas. The sun had just bedded down for the night and, to the west, its last delicate glow coated the tips of the Alps in burnished gold.

They turned and waved to the Satyrs, who looked at them with grave expressions. Finally, one of them bobbed his head and, giving them what Maddock swore was a wistful look, drove his spear into the roof of the tunnel.

There was a flash of blue light, a sound like a grenade exploding, and the roof of the passage caved in. When the dust cleared, only a pile of rocks and rubble remained where the entrance had been.

"Is somebody there?" Angel's voice cut through the night air and, a moment later, a flashlight appeared in the distance. Angel appeared, picking her way along the ridgeline to where Maddock and the others waited.

She crushed Maddock and Bones in a tight embrace, crying and cursing them in turn. She wasn't so rough with Jade, about whom she was clearly worried.

"How did you get here?" Maddock asked.

"I told those douches in town," she pointed down toward the lights, "what happened, but they wouldn't even take a missing person's report at first. Finally, the lady at the inn threw a fit, so they wrote it up, but they insisted the only way under the mountain was through these caverns. The old lady lent me her car and I followed the cops up here. They poked around for a while and then went home." She breathed a deep sigh. "I'm just glad you're all right. You jerks scared the crap out of me running off like that."

"It's all good." Bones assured her. "We're safe and sound, and I've got one hell of a story to tell you when we get back to the pub."

"Well, you don't have to buy me a gift," she said. "You guys getting back safe is enough for me."

"Good thing," Bones said, "because I didn't buy you jack!"

"Ass!" she punched him on the shoulder. "You'd better have gotten me something." Laughing and arguing, they headed back across the ridge, with Maddock and Jade following behind.

Jade looked up at the starry night sky and smiled. "I don't suppose I'll ever think of the Christmas Star the same again."

"Me neither," Maddock agreed. He leaned down and kissed her gently on the lips. "Merry Christmas, Jade."

"Merry Christmas, Maddock."

## End

# AUTHOR'S NOTE

David When I decided to write Icefall, my plan was to write a Christmas-themed short story that I would share with readers on my website. Maddock and Bones had other plans, and my "short story" quickly became a novella. It's much shorter than the usual Maddock adventure, but I'm happy with the way it turned out. I hope you had as much fun reading it as I did writing it.

David

# ABOUT THE AUTHOR

David Wood is the author of the bestselling Dane Maddock Adventures and Dane Maddock Origins series and many other titles. Writing as David Debord, he writes the Absent Gods fantasy series. When not writing he hosts the Wood on Words podcast and co-hosts the Authorcast podcast. David and his family live in Santa Fe,New Mexico. Visit him online at davidwoodweb.com.